Shoot the messenger—before he shoots first . . .

Longarm sat tensely.
and then the man he
walked into the dini
dusty coat and a blac
face, and on his thim
pair of round, iron-rimm

He made a beeline for the table at which Longarm sat
with Spicer and the other Santa Clara town councilmen,
and the bizarre smile that suddenly stretched across his
face made Longarm begin to think he might be a long-
lost acquaintance.

The man strode up to the table and stopped, his fishy
blue eyes looking extra large behind the grime-smeared,
thick lenses of his glasses. "Deputy United States Marshal Custis Long?"

Under the table, Longarm had snaked his right hand
across his belly and released the keeper thong from over
his Colt's hammer. "Who's askin'?"

"Grogan Caulfield, Longarm. Got a message for you
from the Four Horsewomen of the Apocalypse."

The man swept a flap of his black frock coat back
from his hip and, howling like a maniac, raised a sawed-
off, double-barreled shotgun . . .

- ► **TABOR EVANS** ◄ -

LONGARM

AND THE HORSEWOMEN
OF THE APOCALYPSE

JOVE BOOKS, NEW YORK

THE BERKLEY PUBLISHING GROUP
Published by the Penguin Group
Penguin Group (USA) Inc.
375 Hudson Street, New York, New York 10014, USA

Penguin Group (Canada), 90 Eglinton Avenue East, Suite 700, Toronto, Ontario M4P 2Y3, Canada
(a division of Pearson Penguin Canada Inc.)
Penguin Books Ltd., 80 Strand, London WC2R 0RL, England
Penguin Group Ireland, 25 St. Stephen's Green, Dublin 2, Ireland (a division of Penguin Books Ltd.)
Penguin Group (Australia), 250 Camberwell Road, Camberwell, Victoria 3124, Australia
(a division of Pearson Australia Group Pty. Ltd.)
Penguin Books India Pvt. Ltd., 11 Community Centre, Panchsheel Park, New Delhi—110 017, India
Penguin Group (NZ), 67 Apollo Drive, Rosedale, Auckland 0632, New Zealand
(a division of Pearson New Zealand Ltd.)
Penguin Books (South Africa) (Pty.) Ltd., 24 Sturdee Avenue, Rosebank, Johannesburg 2196,
South Africa

Penguin Books Ltd., Registered Offices: 80 Strand, London WC2R 0RL, England

This is a work of fiction. Names, characters, places, and incidents either are the product of the author's imagination or are used fictitiously, and any resemblance to actual persons, living or dead, business establishments, events, or locales is entirely coincidental.

LONGARM AND THE HORSEWOMEN OF THE APOCALYPSE

A Jove Book / published by arrangement with the author

PRINTING HISTORY
Jove edition / September 2011

ISBN: 978-0-515-14989-0

JOVE®
Jove Books are published by The Berkley Publishing Group,
a division of Penguin Group (USA) Inc.,
375 Hudson Street, New York, New York 10014.
JOVE® is a registered trademark of Penguin Group (USA) Inc.
The "J" design is a trademark of Penguin Group (USA) Inc.

PRINTED IN THE UNITED STATES OF AMERICA

10 9 8 7 6 5 4 3 2 1

Chapter 1

"Holy hellfires—look at the *chiconas* on that sweet little Mescin number!" said a tall, red-haired cowboy named Red Hollinbach.

His partner, Giff Clawson, looked up from the beer the rangy cowboy had been sucking the foam from in the little country roadhouse on Massacre Creek nestled in the cactus-carpeted foothills of the Guadalupe Mountains of far West Texas.

"Hot diggidy ding-dong damn!" intoned Clawson, slamming one hand on the table but keeping his voice down as he stared in awe at the four heart-twistingly beautiful young women who'd just now stepped off the tumbleweed-littered front gallery to push through the batwings and saunter toward a table near the doors.

There were three young Anglos and a young Mexican, none much over twenty. All four had their hair fixed in different ways.

One, a hazel-eyed brunette, allowed hers to hang long and in a fetching loose tumble about her slender shoulders, wisps curling toward the rawhide strings that did little to hold her leather vest closed across her alluring cleavage. She wore nothing beneath the vest. Another, a brown-eyed strawberry blonde, wore hers in a French braid secured behind her head with a large silver comb. The third was also a blonde, a blue-eyed wheat blonde; she'd arranged her own shimmering locks in a ponytail hanging straight down her back.

The last, the chocolate-eyed Mexican, had also fashioned a ponytail, a braided one that she'd slid forward over her left shoulder, the ends wrapped in red ribbon and hanging alluringly in the dusky cleavage of her full, tempting bosom, over which her red-and-black calico blouse was pulled taut.

It was this bosomy Mexican maiden whom Hollinbach had been referring to, but that was before he'd seen the other three girls, the two blondes and the brunette, behind her.

It didn't matter that the four women were dressed in the rough but colorful trail garb of West Texas ranch hands, complete with Stetson hats, flare-legged charro slacks trimmed in fancy stitching or hammered silver half-moons and stars, white or calico blouses (aside from the brunette), brush jackets, tooled leather pistol rigs, and high-heeled stockmen's boots with large-roweled silver spurs.

That they were women would be obvious to any living, mildly discerning male over the age of ten from a good quarter-mile across the sotol-bristling Texas desert.

The bartender, Whip Freeman, watched the young women as well as the three Tres Pinos ranch hands who, in turn, watched the four women with unabashed interest. The aging, balding, jowly, apron-clad barman leaned forward against his bar, fat fists atop the scarred plank boards, sliding his gaze between his two sets of customers. Mild amusement shone in his pale blue eyes, and a sly grin pulled at the corners of his mouth.

He didn't get many customers out here at Massacre Creek anymore, since the freight roads that converged here had both been abandoned by better traces to the east and west, skirting Comanche country. All that kept his doors open were the occasional desert drifter and the spur railroad line that passed in front of the place twice a week.

The train only stopped for water, but it paused long enough so that the passengers could journey into the cool shaded depths of the Massacre Creek Saloon to cut the dust and coal smoke from their throats before continuing on to either Stanton to the south or Santa Clara to the north, the little ranch supply towns being a good hundred miles apart.

No, Freeman didn't get much business out here. He was bored most of the time. It was nice to have these three punchers from the Tres Pinos here, drinking beer and whiskey and ogling these girls like maybe one was going to make a play on them and make things even more entertaining.

Hell, Freeman was enjoying ogling these beauties himself.

It was better than swatting flies and waiting on the next train, which wasn't due for several hours.

"Señor—four beers, *por favor*," called the Mexican girl, who'd sat down with her back to the bar while the other three sank into chairs around her, doffing their hats and running hands through their hair or slapping their gloves against their thighs, causing dust to billow.

The Tres Pinos men shared conspiratorial looks as they continued appraising the four lovelies. Billy Honeycutt, the youngest of the three and who had a ratlike, freckled face with a yellow spade beard, elbowed Giff Clawson and snorted tobacco juice out his right mouth corner to dribble into his thin, patchy beard.

Freeman slid his own bemused gaze back to the women and said in his burly baritone, slapping the bar top for emphasis, "Four beers comin' right up, ladies!"

Freeman grabbed four schooners off a back bar shelf, filled them at the spigot protruding from his ten-gallon oak beer cask, and whistling jubilantly, set them on a tray. As he carried the tray to the women's table, he slid his gaze to the three Tres Pinos riders.

The three were still staring at the women, eagerly taking their measure. Billy Honeycutt, who had his back to the front of the room, was staring wide-eyed over his left shoulder. Coffee-colored chaw still oozed from his mouth corner.

Freeman set the beers down in front of the four women, smiling his truckling barman's grin. He himself was having trouble deciding which one of these little gals to focus his attention on. They were equally lovely— even-featured, full-lipped princesses in dusty but well-set-up trail garb that fit them snugly, showing off their best assets. Two wore calico blouses under their brush jackets while the strawberry blonde wore a white silk blouse under a brown, red-stitched brush jacket.

The wheat blonde had the smallest tits, Freeman saw after appraising all four bosoms with a quick, sweeping glance, whistling a little louder as though to distract the women from his gaze. But even hers couldn't be called small. The strawberry blonde's were largest—full and up-tilted with a little silver, turquoise-studded cross nestling inside her alluring, freckled cleavage. The inch-long slanted pink scar on the strawberry blonde's chin did nothing to mar the beauty of her pink-mouthed, tan-eyed face either. Somehow, it enhanced it, gave her allure a slightly savage flavor.

Freeman reflected as he ran his grimy shirtsleeve over a soiled corner of the women's table that if he had to make a choice about which lovely to take upstairs to one of the three rooms he rented to overnighters, he'd likely saw his own head off with a rusty knife in frustration. The Mexican girl with her lustrous dark brown eyes would curl a man's toes, for sure, but the brunette, who was just now staring up at Freeman from beneath her thin brows, while sucking the foam off her beer with swollen lips, was likely a wildcat in the sack. What he wouldn't give to . . .

"*Muchas gracias*, señor." Freeman felt his cheeks warm as he skipped his gaze from the brunette's tits pushing out her red calico blouse, to the Mexican girl staring up at him with her sparkling chocolate eyes and pliant ruby lips stretched in a gracious smile. "What do we owe you, *por favor*?"

Freeman lowered the tray to his stout thigh clad in patched buckskin, and gave a friendly sigh, raising his eyes to the ceiling, as though the bill took him a minute to tally. "Let's see—beer is one nickel. So four beers will run you . . . uh . . . twenty cents! You can pay now or when you're finished imbibin' . . ." He chuckled at his joke.

It was rare for women—at least any of the women he knew besides whores—to ever consume anything stronger than coffee. He'd bet that none of these delicate albeit womanly young creatures could drink one complete beer without passing out. They didn't look like regular beer drinkers. He wasn't sure what they looked like—aside from something from one of his own wet dreams—but they sure as hell weren't beer drinkers.

"Put it on my bill, Whip," said Red Hollinbach, leaning back in his chair and crossing his ankles. He held his own half-drunk beer in both hands on his lap, and his drink-rheumy, cobalt blue eyes were brashly appraising the women.

The women looked at the redheaded puncher.

The strawberry blonde lifted her beer in salute. "Thanks."

"Yeah, thanks," said the wheat blonde.

"*Muchas gracias*, señor," said the Mexican, lifting her own beer above her left shoulder in salute at the man behind her.

"'Preciate it, partner," said the brunette in a sexy, husky rasp, giving her chin a slow, alluring dip then shaking her sexily messy and lustrous hair back behind her shoulders.

"Not a problem," said Red as Freeman walked back behind the bar.

Billy Honeycutt giggled as he turned to Red and sleeved chaw from the scraggly yellow whiskers curling off his pimply chin. Giff Clawson just stared at the women with much the same expression as Red.

Freeman assumed his old position behind the bar, unable to conceal his delight at having his boredom relieved if only for a few minutes of the otherwise long, dusty, hot West Texas afternoon. His heart thudded slightly as Red suddenly gained his feet noisily, kicked his chair back out of his way, took a deep sip from his beer glass, then sauntered over to the girls' table.

"Hi, there," Red said, cocking one scuffed, undershot boot. "I'm Red."

Freeman checked a snort as the four women just looked at him, blank-faced.

Back at Red's own table, his two partners snickered.

Red's ears turned red, and Freeman saw the puncher's shoulders stiffen slightly under his cracked brown leather vest.

The girls looked at him without expression. They didn't say anything.

"I said, the name's Red," the redhead said, louder. "As in Red Hollinbach. Segundo from Tres Pinos."

"Private party," said the girl with the wheat blonde hair and icy blue eyes. "Sorry, Red."

Giff and Billy howled. The four girls continued staring without expression at Red, until Red's ears turned as red as his hair; he pivoted at the hips and sauntered, thoroughly humiliated, back toward his own table.

His partners laughed and howled. Billy slammed his open palm on the table. Red was halfway back to his partners when he swung back around and, the red now fading slightly in his cheeks and neck, sauntered on back to the girls' table and stopped where he'd stood before.

"Don't mean to interrupt," he said boisterously, belligerently, trying to save face, "but I was wondering if you four good-looking little ladies wanna see my snake."

Giff and Billy had piped down when they saw that their partner was going back for more. Now Giff threw his head back and laughed while Billy stared at Red over his shoulder again, chuckling, his eyes wide with unabashed delight.

The girls glanced at each other.

"Snake?" said the Mexican, arching a skeptical brow.

Chapter 2

"*Sí*," said Red, hooking a thumb in his cartridge belt, cocking one foot, and holding his beer down low in his other hand. "I got me a pet snake. A special kinda pet snake. It's a curiosity, fer sure."

The strawberry blonde sipped her beer, swallowed, set her schooner back down on the table, and wiped her mouth with the back of her hand. "Okay, I'll bite— where is this snake, Red?"

Giff and Billy were beside themselves.

Red turned to his partners, beaming.

"It's in my pants," Red said.

"In your pants?" said the wheat blonde, stitching her brows. "That must be a right tame snake, for you to go carryin' it around in your pants, Red."

"Oh, Red!" intoned the Mexican girl, feigning a concerned look. "What if he bites you?"

Red dropped his chin to his chest and laughed while his partners laughed so hard, Billy slapping the table again, that Freeman thought they'd bust the backs off their chairs. The barman himself couldn't help crossing his arms on his chest and sending his own laughter toward the rafters.

"This here snake in my pants," Red said, regaining control of himself and pointing at his crotch, "is tame . . . to a certain extent." His back was facing Freeman, but the barman was fairly certain that Red winked at the girls. "Maybe you'd like to have a look at him—see for yourself what a strange . . . but right *impressive* . . . ole snake he is."

"Dang, Red," said the raspy-voiced brunette, widening her eyes in mock delight, "would you really show us? I get the feelin' your snake ain't somethin' you show around that often, but we'd be pleased as sows snoozin' in mud if you showed it around some. Me and my friends kinda like snakes."

"I do, I do!" said the wheat blonde, sort of jumping and squirming around in her chair. "When I was a little girl, I slept with a pet snake in my bed every night. He curled right up here next to me." She touched her cleavage and gave a slow blink. "But it was just a tame little garden snake. Called 'im Earl. I doubt he was anything like the big snake you got in your pants, Red. Show us, please?"

"I'd love to show you," said Red. "But you're gonna have to come upstairs with ole Red to see his snake. See, Red's snake is kinda shy. Don't like showin' his head in public. Now, if *y'all* wanna come up and have a look—I reckon that'd be all right!"

Freeman was sure he winked at the girls again.

Giff and Billy were bent over in paroxysms of uncontrolled laughter.

"Can we come, too?" Freeman put in, unable to stop

himself. He was having such a damn good time so un-expectedly, he couldn't help joining in.

He was rewarded with a cow-eyed stare from Red.

"How 'bout if you show it to us right here," said the Mexican, turning in her chair to face Red, leaning back with an elbow on the table and hiking a boot on a knee. "You're among friends here, Red."

"I know," said the raspy-voiced brunette, "why don't your friends come over and show us their trouser snakes, too. You know—so we can decide which one each of us fancies." She leaned back in her chair, thrusting her shoulders back, breasts out, and raking Red's crotch with a lusty, tan-eyed stare.

Freeman felt as though a soft female finger had touched his own scrotum.

The blue-eyed blonde continued, "Then, maybe, if we like your snakes well enough, and if they look up to the task, we can all go upstairs together—with a couple bottles of Mr. Freeman's good whiskey, of course—and make a night of it . . ."

Red laughed harder, but then his laughter acquired a hitch before it died altogether. The other two at the other table stopped laughing, as well. Red looked at them, and they both flushed the way he'd been flushing not two minutes before. Billy took another swipe at his goat beard with his shirtsleeve, and sniffed.

"You're joshin'," said Red to the girls.

"Hell if we are," said the wheat blonde.

"Hell if you ain't!"

"Tell your pals to get over here," said the brunette, "and we'll just see if we ain't."

She looked at Giff and Billy, and beckoned. "Come on over here, pards. Hustle them snakes out of your

trousers so's we can get a look at 'em and see if they got
what it's gonna take to accommodate the four randiest,
wildest ladies in all of West Texas on a long, hot West
Texas afternoon." She lifted her beer schooner. "Cheers,
ladies!"

They all clinked glasses and took healthy pulls from
their beers. As they smacked their lips and scrubbed beer
foam from their mouths, they turned expectantly to Red
and Giff and Billy, all three men now looking moder-
ately confused, befuddled. Maybe a little afraid.

"You . . ." Red's voice was halting, and Freeman saw
that his ears were even redder than before. "You wanna
see our trouser snakes . . ."

"You're the one who brought it up," said the strawberry blonde.

"Yeah," said the other three nearly simultaneously.

Red looked at Billy and Giff, both of whom wore expressions of delighted befuddlement. Finally, Red canted
his head, beckoning his two compadres to join him. He
set his beer down on the girls' table, stepped back, and
planted his fists on his hips.

"All right," he said, rising to the unexpected challenge as the other two punchers walked over to him. Giff
and Billy glanced at the girls as though confronting four
bobcats in an insubstantial cage.

Billy was giggling nervously while Giff was poking
the tip of his tongue out of his mustached mouth, grinning stupidly, his eyes bright from the several beers and
whiskey shots he'd consumed over the past two hours. He
puffed his chest out and threw his shoulders back as he
sidled up to Red, pivoting this way and that on his
slender hips.

Billy stopped a few feet from Giff, giggling and cutting his eyes between Red and Giff and the four women watching him and the other two men with grave, faintly challenging looks. Only the raspy-voiced brunette wore the hint of a smile as she sat far back in her chair, chin dipped to her full, ripe bosom.

"You wanna see what we got, eh?" said Giff.

"That's right," said the wheat blonde seriously. "We wanna see what you got, Giff."

"And if you like what you see . . ." said Red.

"If we like what we see," said the chocolate-eyed señorita, "you'll know it." She poked her tongue out of her long, mobile mouth and ran the tip along her lower lip.

"Sh . . . sh . . . shee-it!" stuttered Billy, who'd thought he'd conquered his stuttering several years ago. "I do believe they mean it, fellers!"

Grinning, Red unbuckled his cartridge belt. He let it and his six-gun drop to the floor at his ankles. Seeing that their amigo was indeed confronting the girls' challenge head-on, Giff and Billy followed suit, their own shell belts and .44s dropping to the floor with sharp thuds.

They unbuttoned their pants, and with Red and Giff chuckling and panting and Billy continuing to giggle girlishly, they all three dropped their trousers and threadbare summer underwear, hanging their peckers out for the girls' inspection.

"Holy shit, Billy," said the brunette soberly but quirking one eyebrow in surprise. "You're hung like a Russian race horse!"

The other girls raked their cool gazes across Red's and Giff's dongs and acquired similar expressions as that of the brunette when they saw Billy's sizable chunk of flour white, pink-crowned flesh standing at half-mast from the nest of tangled sandy hair between his legs.

Red's and Giff's grins faded as they followed the girls' gazes to Billy's pecker. Their own eyes widened in shock.

"Holy shit, kid," Giff said under his breath, more than a little indignant.

"You could drive a Baldwin locomotive with a piston that size!" intoned Red, his broad, freckled face crumpling with acrimony.

Freeman had moved far enough down the bar that he could see both the men and the women. He hiked his own brow in surprise. It was true. Billy's organ made Red's and Giff's peckers look like earthworms some younker had dug up to feed the brook trout with.

The barman laughed but choked it back when both Red and Giff sent him a .45 caliber scowl.

"To hell with Red and Giff," said the strawberry blonde, staring hungrily at Billy's dong. "Billy's the one an' only stud horse here!"

"Hey, now!" Red objected.

"Or," said the raspy-voiced brunette, "we could just kill all three of the cold-blooded sonso'bitches."

"You know," said the brunette, sliding her right hand toward the pistol holstered on her right thigh, and unsnapping the gun's keeper thong from over its hammer, "I think that's a better idea."

"Yeah, I reckon," said the wheat blonde, sliding her own ivory-gripped .36 Remington from her soft, leather holster positioned for the crossdraw on her left hip. "That'd suit me just fine. I reckon it'd suit Miss Angie Nordstrom even finer," she added, deepening her voice and hardening her eyes with rage.

Red, Giff, and Billy stood staring at the women in

slack-jawed shock. As all four women gained their feet
with the menacing looks of she-wolves about to spring
on their quarry, they looked at each other as though for
salvation.

Billy was stuttering again. "D-Did you g-gals say
M-M-Miss Angie?"

"That's right," said the strawberry blonde—a muscle
twitched in her perfectly sculpted right cheek, just above
her jaw—"the thirteen-year-old girl from Crossfire Valley you found along the dried-up Saber River last week,
stripped naked, and ravaged mercilessly before turning
her loose to walk home barefoot and naked across the
hot, thorny desert."

"Yeah," said the wheat blonde, twirling her .36 Remy
in her long fingers and pitching her own voice with
menace. "Don't think she probably wanted a look at you
boys' pet snakes—not even Billy's donkey dick—with
which you three depraved bastards tore her up pretty
good inside."

The four women took their positions around the
table, six-shooters in their hands. Wide-eyed, Freeman
shuffled sideways down the bar so he wouldn't catch
one of the bullets he feared were about to fly. Suddenly,
he yearned for a return to his boredom . . .

Red, Giff, and Billy stood still, peckers hanging out,
staring in mute shock at the four iron-wielding maidens
before them. All three Tres Pinos men looked as though
their jaws would break off and tumble to the floor with
their pants and hoglegs.

Giff said in a high-pitched chortle, "Now, you girls
wait, now . . ." He held his hands out in supplication
as he shuffled backward toward the bar, getting his boots
hung up in his pants. "You just *wait*!"

"You wait for this, you sonofabitch," said the raspy-voiced brunette.

All four pistols exploded at once, leaping and roaring in the girls' hands. Covering his head, Freeman ducked down behind the bar from where he couldn't see the carnage—aside from several large spurts of blood mixed with white bone and brains flying against the back bar mirror. But he could hear the seemingly incessant *blam! blam! blams!* of the triggered six-shooters nearly drowning out the men's shrieks and screams and the thudding of their boots as they were driven backward against the bar before slamming to the floor.

When the gunfire died, leaving the thick stench of cordite, silence closed over the saloon.

It was followed nearly a minute later by the clinks of many empty cartridge casings being shaken from pistol cylinders and onto the wooden floorboards.

And the louder crash of several coins being bounced off the bar as boots thudded and spurs rang, one of the kill-crazy women snarling, "We'll pay for our fuckin' beers, amigo!"

Then they left.

Freeman didn't come up from behind the bar until he'd heard the thuds of their galloping horses dwindle into the distance. When he saw the carnage they'd left in their wake, he staggered outside and puked in the horse trough.

Chapter 3

The buxom wife of the mayor of Hangtree Gulch turned to Longarm and said, "I suppose you think that just because you kept those savage Apaches from raping and sodomizing me and staking me out naked and slathered with honey on a hill of ghastly fire ants you'll be allowed certain liberties tonight."

Longarm splashed Maryland rye into his cup of steaming coffee, glanced across the crackling fire at the woman, and poked his coffee brown, flat-brimmed hat back off his forehead. "Oh, I wouldn't count on that, ma'am."

"Oh?" She looked skeptical as she tossed out the blanket roll Longarm had given her to make their desert night sojourn a little more comfortable. She was the only passenger on the stage that the Coyoteros had hit whom he'd managed to save. She'd removed her blouse and wasn't doing anything to conceal the fact that she had a nice load of flesh bouncing around inside her low-cut camisole. "Are you above reproach, Marshal Long?"

"I told ya, ma'am, you might as well call me Longarm since we've been alone together for two days an' all, and likely have another two days' ride back to Hangtree ahead of us. But to answer your question, ma'am—no, I'm far below reproach of nearly any kind imaginable to man, woman, and the beasts of the desert wild. But I will tell you this—if you're thinkin' I'm gonna come over there and give you the roll you're obviously tryin' to lure me into"—he lowered his gaze to her all-but-revealed breasts jostling around in her camisole like plump baby pigs in a gunny sack—"you got another think comin'."

"How dare you!"

"You see," Longarm continued, taking a sip of his piping hot brew laced with rye, which helped steel him against the descending desert chill, "I don't sleep with married women. No, sir. Not even if they're prettier than three spotted pups fightin' over a deer bone in a muddy buffalo wallow."

She sank back against the low rock on the other side of the bed she'd laid out for herself with Longarm's hotroll and saddle, and crossed her arms beneath her breasts. The silver hoop rings dangling from her ears, beneath the rich coil of stygian hair piled loosely atop her fine head, flashed in the firelight. "Is that supposed to be a compliment?"

"Call it what you will. The answer is no."

"As if I'd allow an uncouth saddle tramp like yourself to grunt around between *my* legs! Why, I'd rather give myself to one of those heathen Apaches!"

"Oh, and another thing, Mrs. Banner."

"What's that?"

"Just so's you know."

Longarm set his smoking cup down on a rock beside him and snaked his right hand across his belly, toward the walnut-gripped, double-action Frontier Model Colt holstered for the crossdraw on his left hip.

"Yes?" she said, pitching her voice with impatience.

"You got one o' them heathens behind you right now. But I suggest you sit still as that rock you're leanin' against."

She blinked and stitched her fine brows over her pretty, slanted blue eyes, making a face. "What on earth are you—"

Mrs. Banner broke the question off with her own scream as she turned her head sharply to her left where the brick red, granite-hard face of an Apache warrior had seemed to manifest out of the inky darkness of the Arizona night. The big, handmade knife that the brave was holding and about to slice across the woman's throat flashed brilliantly in the firelight a quarter second before Longarm's Colt leaped and roared, stabbing smoke and bright orange flames across the dancing fire.

The .44 round drilled a quarter-sized hole in the brave's left temple just as he started to bring the knife across Mrs. Banner's neck. Blood sprayed the bole of the tree behind him as he flew back without a yelp, flinging the knife toward the fire, where it clattered against a rock.

Mrs. Banner screamed and splayed her fingers across her throat.

Longarm saw a shadow leap in the darkness just beyond the firelight to Mrs. Banner's left. He swung his double-action pistol in that direction and fired twice more. A rifle flashed, the slug screeching just past Longarm's face as the Indian he'd just shot grunted and bounded back into the deeper darkness beyond the fire.

"I thought you said Apaches won't fight at night!" the woman squealed, staring at him aghast while still clutching her throat as though to make sure it was still intact.

Spying more movement out the corner of his left eye, Longarm rose to a crouch, swinging his pistol around once more and emptying the cylinder, the reports echoing around the rocky hollow he'd bivouacked in after the sun had gone down. The shadow he'd seen to the west had disappeared, but he didn't know if he'd hit the lurking devil.

"I reckon they didn't figure on fightin', just killin'!" Longarm retorted, gritting his teeth as the crunch of moccasins on near gravel sounded on three sides of him, along with the raking breaths of several Apaches running up the northern slope toward the camp.

A figure bolted toward him so quickly that Longarm saw only dark red skin relieved by slanting shadows as well as the war hatchet raised in the running brave's clenched fist. The brave howled like a rabid lobo, dark eyes wide and mouth forming a perfect O as he bore down on the lawman.

"Run upslope!" Longarm shouted to Mrs. Banner as he dropped his empty pistol and ducked, hearing the loud *whoosh!* of the hatchet cutting the air where his head had just been.

The brave grunted as his own momentum swung him nearly completely around. Moving quickly, knowing by the sounds of breathing and running feet that he was badly outnumbered, Longarm looped an arm around the brave's neck and flipped him over his back and shoulders. The brave shrieked as he turned a backward somersault over the lawman's head.

He hit the fire with a crackling thud and the tinny smashing of Longarm's nearly full coffeepot, sparks flying in all directions, spilled coffee sizzling loudly.

The brave squealed and flopped around, trying to throw himself out of the fire while a good three layers of skin burned from his backside.

As Mrs. Banner ran off across the camp and into the firelit rocks marking its southern perimeter, Longarm picked up his empty Colt, grabbed his Winchester from the bleached log he'd leaned it against, and ran into the rocks behind the fleeing woman.

"Run and keep running till I tell you to stop!" Longarm shouted at her retreating silhouette.

He himself stopped at the edge of the firelight, shouldered up against the side of a wagon-sized boulder, racked a live cartridge into his rifle's breech, raised the stock to his shoulder, and aimed into the camp, where three Apaches clad in only loincloths, moccasins, and red calico bandannas were just now bounding in from the northern slope.

Two were armed with Spencer carbines hanging from leather lanyards around their necks. The third had a knocked bow and arrow. Longarm waited until all three were inside the sphere of firelight then cut loose with the Winchester, sending all three backpedaling and twisting and screaming, blood spewing from the wounds in their chests and bellies, in the direction from which they'd come.

Judging from the yowls rising behind them, as though the area around the encampment were suddenly besieged with kill-crazy, otherworldly demons, there were plenty more in the war party those three and the others had come from.

Likely, the bronco band of reservation-jumping Apaches that had been attacking stagecoaches running between Hangtree and Lordsburg had not taken lightly to Long-

arm and his four now-deceased lawdogging colleagues'
drawing a line in the Sonoran sand and killing a good
dozen of the Apaches after they'd attacked the last stage
and taken Mrs. Banner hostage.

Longarm had rescued the mayor of Hangtree's wife
and killed three Apaches at their encampment, when
the others had been off hunting or some such. But here
those others were now—with a vengeance.

Longarm ejected a hot cartridge casing and whipped
around to start running up the hill, grinding his teeth
against having to give up his horse and the horse he'd
stolen for the woman. But he'd tied the horses on the
downslope, and there was no way that he could get to
them now.

Running hard, he quickly overtook the tiring Mrs.
Banner and grabbed her arm and pulled her along behind him. She sobbed and groaned and then gasped when
she heard the Apaches behind them giving a harrowing
yell, triggering several more shots. The bullets ricocheted
off the rocks around Longarm and the woman, one chew-
ing into a one-armed saguaro left of the faint game trail
they were on.

There was no moon, so Longarm had to navigate by
starlight. It helped that the boulders and sand were red;
they reflected the starlight well enough that he had a
pretty clear sense of the trail winding up the slope toward a rocky spine.

Behind him, he could hear the foot thuds of running
Apaches. The braves fired occasional shots but they obviously could not see their quarry, because most of the
bullets flew wild.

When he was virtually dragging the woman on her
knees behind him, Longarm turned off the trail and

stopped. He released Mrs. Banner's arm, and she fell to her hands and knees, crying openly from shock and exhaustion. Longarm dropped to his own knees and peered through a gap in the rocks, seeing the man-shaped shadows running hard along the trail snaking up the incline around boulders and cactus snags.

The desert night was so still and quiet that he could clearly hear them breathing and grunting with each pump of their elbows and knees.

Longarm thumbed back his Winchester's hammer, laid his sights on the nearest Apache, and fired. The brave gave an agonized whoop as he flung both arms into the air above his head, hurling away his carbine, and flew sideways into the rocks and out of sight.

Longarm stretched his lips with a hard satisfaction and drew down on the next brave, who'd been running about ten yards behind the first. Just as this brave began to slow his pursuit and swing his head around cautiously, Longarm gave him the same treatment as the last.

He ejected the spent cartridge, hearing the second brave groan and scramble weakly around in the brush, his breath sounding liquid, and saw the straggly line of several others stop suddenly, break, and duck behind boulders, shrubs, and cactus.

Longarm stared down the slope toward the flickering light of his and the woman's fire mostly concealed by the large boulders that were blocky silhouettes against it. He could hear the Apaches moving furtively around down there, but he saw no shadows running up the incline toward him.

He'd held them off. For now.

He looked around, then grabbed the sobbing woman's arm once more, and jerked her to her feet. "Let's go."

"Oh, God—no. I can't run another step!"

"Shut up," he grated out as he began pulling her along behind him and tracing a meandering course through the brush and rocks, continuing upslope toward the rocky ridge.

At the ridge crest, Longarm stopped.

"Ah, shit."

"What is it?" the woman said, breathless.

She lifted her head to peer into the canyon yawning below. A good hundred feet down there appeared a giant, shiny black snake slithering through the gorge. Only it wasn't a snake. It was water.

The gorge held a river.

"Well, now what are we going to do?" Mrs. Banner said accusingly.

Just then, Longarm heard running footsteps. They grew louder. He and the woman were behind large rocks, so he couldn't see the Apaches. He didn't need to. They were coming hard, leaping rocks and brush. From their savage, eager grunts and jubilant howls, they likely knew they had their quarry trapped between themselves and the river, and they were throwing caution to the wind.

"There's really only one thing we can do," Longarm said reasonably.

"What's *that*?" the woman fairly screamed.

"Jump."

She planted her feet in their canvas half-boots with their side buttons and too-high heels and extended her neck to look down at those glistening oily depths. "Are you *mad*?"

She'd just started to lurch away from him when he got a good hold on her arm and stepped off the cliff into empty air.

Chapter 4

Nearly three weeks later, Longarm pushed through the door in the Denver Federal Building marked CHIEF MARSHAL WILLIAM VAIL, Denver First District Court, and tossed his hat on the antler hat tree just inside the chief marshal's outer office. "How's it hangin', Henry?"

The prim little bespectacled gent sitting behind the desk to Longarm's left and banging on one of them new-fangled typing machines on a smaller desk abutting the far left wall turned a bored look over his shoulder, thumbed his spectacles up his pale nose, and sniffed. "You're late, Marshal Long." Turning forward again to face the typing machine once more, which he promptly resumed hammering away on, he added, "Go on in. The chief marshal is waiting for you . . . as usual."

"Ah, come on, Henry. Don't give me that coyote stare. You know my vacation ain't over."

Longarm stopped in front of the young man's carefully arranged desk, manilla folders stacked neatly on one side, cloth-bound ledger books stacked neatly on the other side, and all presided over by a goose-necked green-shaded Tiffany lamp.

"Look here." Longarm drummed the fingers of his left hand on his right forearm, indicating that the entire appendage was still suspended by a white cotton sling. "My wing ain't even healed yet. You don't mean to tell me that Billy thinks he gonna throw this broken bird to the wolves again so soon, when my leave ain't over and I'm still injured from a long hard ride down an Arizona canyon rapids with a howlin' woman on my back!"

"On your back? That shouldn't be an entirely new position for you." Henry puffed out his pasty cheeks in a snort of sorts while his eyes remained deadpan.

Longarm opened his mouth to respond but closed it again when the frosted-glass paned door of Billy Vail's office opened, and the boss himself stuck his round, nearly bald head out. "Custis, if you're done bothering Henry with your consarned bellyachin', get in here. You're six minutes late."

"I ain't done yet, Billy."

"Get in here!"

Billy turned and walked back into his office. Scowling like a schoolboy caught talking in class, Longarm went in and closed the door on which Billy's name was etched in gold leaf lettering. There was the usual cloud of cheap cigar smoke hovering over Billy's desk the size of a Murphy freight wagon bed and so cluttered that Longarm didn't doubt that several generations of rats had been raised in and around it without Billy noticing a one. Two hefty ashtrays, one cut glass and one wood carved into the shape of a bear claw, spilled stogie butts resembling squashed Pacific Coast banana slugs.

Billy stood near the door looking pudgy and dumpy,

one white shirttail hanging out of his broadcloth trousers. He gave Longarm's sling-suspended arm a whack with the back of the hand holding another half-smoked stogie.

"How's your arm doing?" the chief marshal asked his deputy, an oblique glint in his washed-out blue eyes.

"It hurts!"

"Really?" Billy smacked the arm again, harder. "How 'bout that?"

Longarm looked indignant as he stared down at the stocky little man, who was a good six inches shorter than his subordinate's six-foot-four. "Ow!"

"You poor fuckin' thing!"

"What's the meaning of this, Billy? If you called me out of my rented digs over on the poor side of Cherry Creek just to aggravate the injuries I acquired in that last damn-near-fatal assignment you gave me, I reckon I'll just head on back to bed and finish recovering. You've obviously been drinking, and I don't—"

"Back to bed, huh?" Billy rose onto the balls of his scuffed brogans, grinning up at Longarm. "Who you got back there, Custis? It wouldn't be one Cynthia Larimer, would it? The apple of General William H. Larimer's eye? You know the general—the one who founded this here little cow town in the first fuckin' place? The important man whose niece you've been screwin' in every orifice for the past three years *seven ways from sundown*?"

"Wha—*huh*?"

"His niece, as you know better than anyone, is Miss Cynthia Larimer, the reigning queen of Denver—all tits and cobalt blues and dick-sucking lips, and with whom you were seen prowling around Sixteenth Street as well as Larimer Street last night until nearly four o'clock this morning."

Billy gave Longarm's injured wing another slug as he stared up at the tall deputy with a devilish grin.

"From eyewitness accounts, it seems your right arm was not only minus this here sling but it was allowing you to lift beer schooners every which way as well as that little Larimer vixen's delightful little ass in an' out of rented hacks. My friend and poker partner, attorney Mort Sheffield, says he even seen you two waltzing together over at the Larimer ballroom—pardon the pun!— and raising this here poor injured wing of yours a good three feet above your head!"

"Billy, goddamnit," Longarm raged with self-righteous indignation, whipping the sling off his arm and throwing it down on the floor at his boss's feet. "Were you *spying* on me?"

"You're smarter than you look. Wish I could say I set out to do it, but no, I believed your malarkey about that injured wing. It wasn't till I met up with Sheffield this morning over breakfast at the Black Cat that I learned about your all-night prowl and likely your all-morning mattress dance with Miss Larimer."

Longarm cursed. He'd seen the dapper, shifty-eyed attorney and acquaintance of Billy's out last night with his cronies and several women of ill repute. The big lawman should have known the mousy little law reader would inform Billy. Should have dragged him into an alley and threatened him at gunpoint.

"All right, I admit me and Cynthia went out on the town last night. But the arm wasn't malarkey. I damn near had it twisted plum off in that river whilst I was trying to keep the mayor of Hangtree's wife's head above the raging current. It was sprained, Billy, and just started feelin' better a few days ago. I told you it was still hurtin' because I knew you would have tried cutting my vacation—my *hard-earned* vacation—short if you'd thought it was fully healed."

Billy walked back behind his desk. "You're right, I'm cutting it short."

"Billy, you know how long it's been since I've had two weeks off?"

"Yes, I do. Too long. Way too long." Billy chuckled with self-satisfaction and plopped down in his high-backed, overstuffed, leather swivel chair, puffing his stogie. "Remind me when you've returned from Texas, and I'll see if I can sneak you another couple of days though why I would after catching you in that school-yard lie is far beyond me!"

The scowl lines in Longarm's saddle brown forehead deepened. "Texas! Billy, you can't send me to Texas in the middle of the goddamned summer!"

"Christ, you balk at being sent to Dakota Territory in the winter and Texas in the summer. Why don't you just write out for me where you will and will not go and when, and I'll use it for tinder next time I need to light my stove." He picked up a sheet of paper from a sheath before him, and tossed it across his desk to Longarm, who caught it out of the air one-handed. "Oh, before I forget . . ."

"What's this?"

"Letter from one Mrs. Olivia Banner from Hangtree, Arizona."

Longarm's ears warmed with chagrin.

"What's the matter?" Billy said, apparently seeing the guilty look on Longarm's face. "Seems the woman appreciated how you saved her from them Apaches and that river, and wrote a long letter praising you and even requesting that you be given some sort of award—a ribbon or a plaque or some such. Even said she'd like to be here for the, uh, *ceremony*."

Billy grinned.

"Damn nice of her," Longarm said, not bothering to read the woman's feminine script laid out nicely on the cream parchment paper, but tossing it back over to his boss. "How 'bout if you just pay me in cash or Maryland rye?"

"How 'bout if you quit fucking married women?"

Longarm didn't know how to respond to that. Sometimes he thought that his boss knew the inside of Longarm's mind better than Longarm himself did. The rangy deputy blinked as he stared through the wafting smoke at Billy.

"Billy, you're crazier'n a tree full of owls."

"You did, didn't you?" The chief marshal was grinning again—that cunning, knowing grin. "You bedded the mayor of Hangtree's pious wife."

Not so pious, Longarm thought, unable to extinguish the image of him and the woman rolling around together on that warm, sandy beach after they'd finally made it through the rapids intact. The water had slowed and grown shallower as the tall banks had pulled away. Longarm and the woman had slogged arm in arm to the shore and lay there for a long time, half-conscious, dozing from the exhaustion of the wet, violent tumult.

They'd known that not even the vengeance-hungry Apaches, rugged aborigines of the desert mountains, would follow them down the river or downstream along the treacherous canyon ridge from where their desperate quarry had leaped into the stream a good mile or more away from their current location, just above the rapids. Not in the dark they wouldn't. Probably not even during the day.

When Longarm had rolled onto his back, he'd looked up. Mrs. Banner was staring down at him. Her head was silhouetted against the twinkling, starry sky. She wore an unreadable expression on her pretty face that was pale from their near-demise at the hands of the Apaches as well as the raging river. Her coal black hair was pasted against her face and neck. She'd lost an earring. Her camisole was soaked and torn, exposing nearly all of one full breast, the large aureole and pink nipple of which were visible inside the tear, touched with starlight.

Both breasts rose and fell heavily as she stared down at him, her lips seeming to grow fuller and fuller as she stared. She ran her hand down the length of her tapering thigh, kneading it anxiously through the clinging fabric, as she raked the big man with her gaze. Longarm's shirt had been torn open in their free fall down the rapids, exposing his broad, hard-muscled chest, washboard belly, and one shoulder as large and round as a wheel hub.

Despite the desert chill and the ache in his all-but-dislocated arm, Longarm felt a hot surge in his loins. He'd reached up, grabbed the woman around her neck, kissed her hard for a time before he ripped the camisole apart with his fists, exposing both breasts.

He shoved her back against the damp sand, and took her over and over again until finally, in the early hours of the next morning, they slept naked and entangled.

How in the devil's red hell did Billy know?

"Okay, you got me, ya old mossyhorn. But let me say this in my defense—she ain't near as pious as you'd think." Longarm grinned and glanced down at the letter Mrs. Banner had sent to Billy. "And I reckon she was, uh, satisfied on all counts."

"Yeah, I reckon that'll go in your file, you fortunate bastard. Reckon this proves the Almighty really does watch out for fools, don't he? But I swear if General Larimer don't shoot you with one o' his foreign-made bird guns, Mr. Banner likely will . . . if you was ever to show your face back in Hangtree, that is."

"I got no plans to head back to Arizona Territory anytime soon."

"No, not Arizona." Billy took another deep puff off his cigar, and grinned again delightedly. "West Texas. Damn, but I bet it's hot down there this time of the year. Likely damn near as hot as Arizona."

Longarm shook his head. "You got a mean streak, Billy. What the hell's goin' on down West Texas way anyway? Mescins runnin' stolen cattle across the Rio Grande again? Can't they wait till winter, fer Chris-sakes?"

"Nope. That ain't it. This is a strange one. And the reason I'm assigning you is because it's right up your alley, since it seems to involve four beautiful albeit ne-farious women, an' all."

Longarm reached inside his black frock coat and dug a three-for-a-nickel cheroot and stove match out of the breast pocket of his white dress shirt recently washed and starched by a Chinese laundry on Larimer Street. "Beautiful, nefarious women?" Longarm poked the cheroot between his teeth and scratched the match to life on his thumbnail. "Damn, Billy, those are my favorite kind!"

"Figured you'd say that."

"What kinds of federal problems are the beautiful, nefarious women causing down West Texas way?"

"All kinds. Last week they killed three cowpunchers from a big English ranch run by Bart Spicer—former Texas Ranger who was crippled sometime ago in a stampede. One of the men these women killed was Spicer's segundo, Red Hollinbach. Bart misses Red. Red was a damn good segundo."

"Still don't see how it's federal."

Billy sent another heavy smoke puff washing into the fetid air over his desk, squinting one eye and holding up a waylaying hand. "Bart wrote me a letter requesting my assistance in the matter. Bart an' me go back a ways, all the way back to the Injun wars before the Little Misunderstandin' broke out between the States. What makes our assistance within the boundaries of our jurisdiction is that these four kill-crazy bitches held up a stagecoach a few weeks back—one that was carryin' the U.S. Mail.

"Now, that was the only time they messed with anything federal. Otherwise, they just been killin' cowboys and drummers an' such and stealin' strongboxes haulin' plain old dinero. But since they messed with the mail, if even that one time, no one's gonna give this office any grief for goin' in and sniffin' around and seein' if *you* can run these Four Horsewomen of the Apocalypse to ground, and throw the book at 'em."

"What'd you call 'em?"

"That's what they call themselves when they leave callin' cards layin' around a crime scene—the Four Horsewomen of the Apocalypse." Billy snorted caustically.

Longarm studied the smoking end of his long, black cheroot. "Billy, you mean to tell me the local law can't throw the long loop on these gals?"

"Oh, I don't know—maybe they could," Billy said, "if *he* wasn't *dead*! Yessir, they killed the marshal of town at the center of their rampage—Santa Clara— when he led a posse out after 'em when they held up a stage last month. Shot him right out of his saddle and dumped his body onto a well-traveled stage road with a sign hangin' around his neck announcin', 'Compliments of the Four Horsewomen of the Apocalypse.' Merciless bitches." Billy shook his head. "Awful when you can't depend on the kindness, tenderness, and respectability of the fairer sex."

Billy gave a grim, what's-the-world-coming-to sigh and took another puff from his stogie. "The county sheriff's been after these gals, but it's a vast county nestled there in the foothills of the Guadalupe Mountains, and he's got only two deputies, and they're mostly tied up with Mexican cattle rustlers. There's a couple of cavalry outposts out that way, but you know what kind of investigators the Army makes, and they're busy with bronco Comanches. You're gonna have to go out there and put your experience to work, sniffin' 'em out. Spicer thinks these girls are holed up somewhere in the Guadalupes. Only come down to mame, kill, and steal money from banks, stagecoaches, and the occasional wealthy ranch house."

"No one's got any idea who they are?"

"Nope."

"They kill men *and* women?"

Billy glanced thoughtfully down at his desk. "I believe they've killed only men so far."

Longarm frowned.

Billy sniffed and thumbed his glasses up his nose. "Can't even get much of a description on 'em. Oh, they've been seen aplenty, but it seems they're so god-damn good-looking that no one really *notices* 'em—if you get my drift. It's almost as if they're wearin' *pretty veils*, or some such."

Longarm stared pensively through his own wafting cigar smoke, and thought about that. He had to admit, if only to himself, that it was rather hard to truly see the details of a beautiful woman—aside from her sexual attributes, that was. He wondered why that should be . . . It was almost as if beauty was somehow hard to see past, like a jewel that gave off a blinding glare.

"Anyway," Billy said, "here's the file." He closed the open file folder in front of him, and tossed it onto the edge of his desk, in front of Longarm. "Take this and beat it. Read it on the train." He glanced at the banjo clock on his wall. "You got forty-five minutes to hop the flier to Santa Clara!"

"Thanks for all the extra time!"

"Oh, and one more thing."

Longarm had grabbed the file and was scrambling for the door to the outer office. He turned with his hand on the knob, and looked back over his shoulder at his boss.

Billy wore a sober expression, washed-out blue eyes hooded, his sandy brows stitched. "I got a bad feelin' about this one, Custis. I joke about you and that incorrigible pecker of yours. But this time it really *could* be the end of you."

"What're you sayin', Billy?"

"Keep it in your pants!"

Chapter 5

Delbert Henry McKinley stared down the barrel of his
Winchester repeater into the deep canyon below him,
and clicked the hammer back. He drew a bead on the
broad, sun-leathered forehead of the man at the head of
the five-man contingent of Army payroll guards, and
squeezed the trigger.

The Army sergeant's head fairly exploded as the .44
slug plowed through it, spraying blood across the big
bay of the corporal riding off his own sorrel's right hip.
McKinley did not wait for the sergeant to tumble life-
lessly off his horse.

Hearing the guns of his cohorts, Melvin Little Bear
and Snake Demarest, explode in the rocks along the
canyon ridge to his right, he cocked the Winchester
again quickly and took aim at the freckled forehead of a
private riding to the right of the pack mule carrying the
strongbox. Just as the private opened his mouth to yell,
fumbling his Army Colt from his black leather holster,

McKinley drilled the young man through the middle of his blue, gold-buttoned tunic.

The killer grinned as he ejected the spent shell casing and seated a fresh one in the Winchester's chamber, pressing his cheek against the walnut stock once more as he slid the barrel around, looking for another target. He saw nothing but tumbling soldiers, bucking horses, and wafting dust.

To his right, a rifle thundered once more. A shrill whinny rose as the horse carrying the strongbox curveted suddenly, and tumbled onto its right side, hooves scissoring.

"Good thinkin', Snake!" McKinley said, hauling himself to his feet.

He stared into the canyon. All five soldiers were down. Only two were moving, writhing and groaning in agony.

He and his two cohorts scrambled along the ridge to the trail that twisted down the steep slope, and went slipping and sliding along the trace, grabbing rocks and wiry shrubs to break their falls. McKinley's heart thudded heavily. He'd been waiting for a take as large as this Army payroll for a long time. He'd grown tired of the slim pickings the gang had gleaned from the occasional traveling drummer or stagecoach.

They just weren't worth the risk. Why, only two weeks ago, his twin brother, Jake, got cut in half by a shotgun rider's double-bore coach gun. And all that the gang had hauled down that day was twenty-six dollars in loose change and greenbacks and a pearl-handled hairbrush!

With forty thousand dollars padding their pockets, McKinley and the fellers could live a good, long time down in Old Mexico, drinking and tumbling with the putas around Monterrey! Of course, McKinley would honor his brother's memory. But what better way to honor it than by grunting between the spread knees of a dusky-skinned señorita?

Wouldn't Jake have done the same for him?

As he gained the bottom of the canyon, McKinley swept his gaze along the canyon floor. One of the soldiers was trying to crawl off up the dry water course, belly down and pushing himself along with his legs while clamping a hand against his side. McKinley could hear his raspy breath and his grunts through gritted teeth—a lean, tow-headed kid with a rooster tail.

The horse that had been hauling the strongbox lay still, eyes open, rubbery lips stretched back from its yellow teeth. Beyond it, one more soldier lay squirming and clutching his bloody guts, sobbing and cursing.

McKinley glanced at the big half-breed, Melvin Little Bear, who stood to his left, then tossed his head at the soldier crawling up canyon. As Little Bear levered a live round into his Spencer's breech and began striding up canyon, McKinley walked around the dead packhorse, his eyes glued to the iron-banded strongbox still strapped to its back but now lying on its side with a big padlock showing. McKinley stood over the gut-shot soldier— a broad-faced lieutenant wearing a sweeping dragoon mustache but who was little older than the corporal McKinley had shot from the ridge.

"D-Don't," the young man begged. "Please, don't—"

McKinley clipped the lieutenant's plea with a .44 round through his forehead. The lieutenant's head jumped violently, blood bubbling up from the gaping hole, then turned to one side, the lids of both eyes drooping but not quite closing. His bloody hands fell away from his belly.

A second later, Little Bear's rifle barked, the report echoing sharply off the canyon's rocky walls. The rasps of the other wounded soldiers stopped abruptly.

"Good Lord, fellas, lookee here!"

Snake Demarest was down on his hands and knees and crouched over the strongbox strapped to the dead horse, caressing the side of the wooden box as though it were a newborn baby.

"Oh, Lordy . . . Lordy, Lordy, Lordy!"

"Holy shit, Snake, don't fuck the goddamn thing. If you can peel yourself away for a few seconds"—McKinley loudly racked another .44 round—"I'll blow the lock off and we get to the goodies *inside*!"

Snake peeled himself away from the strongbox, and as Melvin Little Bear walked up in his sullen, Indian way, coal black eyes betraying no emotion whatever, McKinley blew the lock off the box. Snake dropped to both knees, chuckling, and tossed his rifle aside. He burned his fingers on the lock before he managed to free it from the box's hasp. Undeterred, he lifted the lid. McKinley knelt beside him, and both men shoved their hands into the box, bringing up two fistfuls each of banded twenty-dollar greenbacks.

They laughed and yowled.

Little Bear knelt down then, too, and while not show- ing any emotion on his face, McKinley could hear the big half-breed breathing hard as he dipped his own big, dark hands into the box and pulled out two paper- wrapped bundles. He raised them to his face and closed his eyes as he sniffed.

"Damn, Melvin," McKinley said, "you ever see so

much dinero in one place in your entire half-breed life?"

Little Bear was still sniffing the two stacks of bills when McKinley and Demarest dumped all the money out of the box and began counting the bundles of twenty-dollar bank notes. McKinley had calculated close to thirty thousand dollars when something drew his attention to Little Bear.

The big half-breed still held the two bundles up to his nose, but he was staring over them and down canyon on McKinley's right. A wind had come up, blowing dust around the three outlaws and the dead soldiers and packhorse, sliding Melvin's black hair back away from his broad, flat, hawk-nosed red face, which was the color of scorched sandstone.

The corners of his eyes wrinkled with mute interest.

McKinley followed Little Bear's gaze down canyon, and stitched his shaggy red-brown eyebrows together. He'd obviously had too much to drink on the ride out here to set up the ambush on the payroll guards. Or he'd gotten too much sun and was hallucinating . . .

McKinley blinked his eyes and shook his head as if to clear the mirage from behind his retinas. Didn't work. The four beautiful, pistol-hung women were still there, standing side by side along the canyon floor, gloved fists on their hips, staring stonily at the three outlaws. All four wore tan or cream dusters and billowy neckerchiefs, and the dusters flapped out around them in the dusty breeze, like wings.

Snake Demarest sensed that his two accomplices' attention was no longer on the money, and followed their gazes to the women.

"Holy shit!" Snaked dropped the money in his hands

and straightened with a jerk, stumbling backward in shock and poking his hat brim back off his forehead. "Where'd you gals come from?"

McKinley straightened slowly. Little Bear remained on his knees, slowly lowering the two bundles of green-backs in his hands to the ground.

The women said nothing, only stared at the three outlaws, fists on their hips near their holstered six-shooters.

"What'd you want?" McKinley said, his heart quick-ening with apprehension.

Snake jerked a frenetic look at him. "They seen us, Del. Now what in the hell we gonna do?"

McKinley licked his lips. He still wasn't entirely sure the four women were not a figment of his imagination. A waking wet dream. They were four of the most beautiful young women he'd ever laid his eyes on. Still, he could feel chicken flesh rising on the back of his neck.

He pointed at them, narrowing one eye. "If you think we're sharing any of this with you gals, you got another think comin'!"

"We don't want to share it," said one of the women— a raspy-voiced, hazel-eyed brunette who wore a dark green broad-brimmed felt Stetson. She wore a gold locket studded with a single turquoise bead around her neck. Her lips were wide and red against the light tan of her perfectly smooth face and tan eyes flashing copper. Her lips stretched into a slow, menacing grin.

The others—two blondes and a Mexican gal with long hair woven into a long braid curling forward over her left shoulder—smiled then, as well.

"No, no, no," said the Mexican girl. "We do not share, amigos."

"We want it all," said the blue-eyed blonde.

"Every fuckin' bill," said the brown-eyed strawberry blonde wearing a black hat banded with silver conchos, and a long, cream duster.

Melvin Little Bear rose slowly, knees creaking softly as they straightened.

"Well," said Snake with a wary hitch in his voice then chuckling to cover it, "like Del here said—you got another think comin'! Tell you what we will do, though. We'll let you ride our peckers for a hundred split up between the four of yas."

The four women glanced at each other. The strawberry blonde dropped her chin, chuckling and running her thumb across her nose. The others laughed then, too. It wasn't a pretty sound.

"How 'bout if you three go fuck each other in hell?" said the raspy-voice brunette through a sudden, savage snarl.

McKinley and Snake Demarest opened their mouths to scream at the same time while reaching for the six-shooters on their hips. Before either one could even begin to snake their guns free of the leather, all they could see before them was red fire and wafting smoke.

Bullets hammered through them and the big half-breed, punching them straight back off their feet.

Before they even hit the ground, the cold, silent darkness had descended.

Chapter 6

Longarm fired up a three-for-a-nickel cheroot and watched out the dust-streaked window of the shabby coach car he'd spent the last two days in as the little town of Santa Clara slid into view along the railroad tracks.

The town sat perpendicular to the tracks, so Longarm could see nearly straight down the broad, dusty main street. The craggy, sun-blasted humps of the Guadalupe Range rose beyond the town, offering a break from the hot winds blowing over the range from the western New Mexico badlands. The town itself was larger than Longarm would have expected for this far off the beaten path.

As the coach car squawked and jerked to a gradual halt in front of the little train station perched on a dirt lot and framed by telegraph poles running from north to south along the tracks, he could see another frame building calling itself The Santa Clara Cattleman's Association. Beyond it, in adobe brick or stone or brush-roofed mud shacks, were a bank, a stage depot, a hardware shop, a general store, a drugstore, and a women's clothing shop. A low, shingle-roofed stone building housed the town marshal's office. There appeared to be two hotels, a café, a doctor's office, a dentist, a bathhouse, and three saloons. A punctuating afterthought, a steepled white church stood like a glaring, admonishing sentinel at the town's far end.

Flanking both lines of false-fronted main street buildings were private dwellings of every shape and size, most little more than mud shacks with attached chicken or goat pens. There were a few frame houses surrounded by white picket fences and flanked by prim privies and buggy sheds.

But most of the dwellings were the far humbler affairs left over from Santa Clara's early days when the population consisted mostly of Mexicans whose families had probably been there for several generations, when Santa Clara was still part of Old Mexico, before the sacking of the Alamo. There was an old mud-brick well and an old Spanish church grown up with sage and ocotillo though the well-worn, flour white path leading to its front door said it was still being used. The stone shack behind it, abutted by a sun-blistered, wooden stock pen, was probably where the priest resided.

Longarm detrained with a good many others, most of whom had the lanky, sun-seasoned look of cowpunchers, some with the dusky hues and sweeping black mustaches of Spanish descent. The town was close enough to the Goodnight-Loving cattle trail that it probably picked up a good bit of business from itinerate drovers sweeping the area ranches for work.

"You must be Longarm," said one of the three men who'd been sitting on a bench in front of the depot building and who were now strolling through the small crowd toward the rangy federal lawman. "Mr. Spicer informed us that likely the tallest man stepping off the train, and one wearing a big longhorn mustache with a long, thin cigar poking out of it, would be the man we've been waiting for."

Longarm dropped his war bag and let the man, stoop-shouldered and with thinning hair, pump his lone free hand. He had his new McClellan saddle, saddlebags, and sheathed Winchester '73 propped on his right shoulder. He puffed smoke around the stogie between his lips as he frowned at the stoop-shouldered man who'd spoken, as well as the other two.

"Don't believe I ever met Mr. Spicer."

"Said he's met you. Or at least seen you over in Abilene, a few years ago, takin' down a coupla owlhoots right out in the street. He was quite sure you were the man we were looking for. Said he requested you special from Chief Marshal Billy Vail's office up in Denver."

"You have me at a disadvantage," Longarm told the stoop-shouldered gent, who wore a gray serge coat over a crisp white shirt.

He introduced himself as Madison Pringle, owner of the Guadalupe House. The stocky, bearded gent in a pinstriped suit, eye monocle, and pearl-handled walking stick, and who spoke with a slight German accent, was the town mayor, Mortimer Braun. The tall, slender man with red muttonchops and wearing a crisp black claw-hammer coat was W. Angus Whitehurst. Even if he hadn't introduced himself as the president of the Santa Clara Bank & Trust, Longarm would have guessed it. Braun had a banker's fishy handshake and a smile that looked as though it might crack his broad, bearded cheeks, which appeared sallow beneath the bright pink of a recent sunburn.

Longarm hadn't thought bankers were ever in the sun long enough to get burned.

Pringle and Whitehurst were on the four-man town council, with Braun, the mayor, being the third. Not an unusual setup in backwater settlements spotting the wild frontier.

"Shall we mosey over to the hotel?" Pringle asked, when Longarm had shaken hands all around. "I've reserved a table. Thought you might like a bite to eat after your long journey, Deputy Long. And perhaps a libation or two? Meanwhile, we can discuss the most vexing, uh, *situation* we currently find ourselves in."

"You mean them women?"

The three men flushed and lowered their eyes, obviously embarrassed to have been brought to heel by four of the fairer sex.

"Yes," Pringle said, chagrined. "The four young ladies running as wild around here, stirring up as much trouble, as any loco Kiowa."

"You got Maryland rye over to your hotel, Mr. Pringle?"

"Why, yes, I believe I do, Deputy Long."

Longarm grinned and rolled his cheroot from one side of his mouth to the other. "Then lead the way!"

As Longarm reached for his war bag, he thought maybe one of the three Santa Clara boosters might offer to give him a hand. But all three, oblivious of the federal's need or merely too highfalutin to tote luggage for a wage earner, quickly turned and began strolling off around the depot building as Longarm was left to lug all his gear himself.

As he walked, he noticed an unpainted gallows platform standing near the Kelly Mercantile on the west side of the street, about a block away. Four nooses dangled from a crossbeam toward four trapdoors in the whipsawed boards of the floor suspended five feet off the ground. He tossed his head toward it. "That for the current gang of troublemakers?"

"It is now," said Pringle. "Our old marshal, Arden Anderson, had it built a couple years ago as sort of a warning to them that might think about breaking the laws here in Santa Clara. It's always been rough around here, ya see, and that grisly contraption has come in handy. Wasn't built *specifically* for those four demon females, but it's sure gonna come in handy again when we . . . er, *you* . . . run 'em to ground!"

The rangy federal was pondering that, grunting under the weight of his gear while puffing his long, black cheroot, when a train whistle sounded along the tracks behind him and west. He turned to see what appeared to be a miniature locomotive—fully half the size of a regular one—puff and clatter into view from the rolling, cactus-studded desert. There were only two cars behind the small, black and brass locomotive—a tender car heaped with split firewood, and a fancily appointed coach car with brass rails on the vestibules and a little brass chimney poking out of the corrugated tin roof.

Along the glistening yellow side of the car, stenciled in blocky, ornate red script beneath the windows were the words TRES PINOS LAND AND CATTLE COMPANY, LTD.

"Ah, I had a feeling Mr. Spicer would be joining us," said Madison Pringle as he, Braun, and Whitehurst stopped to regard the ornate little train. "He's the fourth member of the town council, and since Tres Pinos is the largest spread around, Spicer likes to keep a close watch over all the town's doings."

There was more than a touch of sarcasm in Pringle's voice.

As the combination pulled to a stop in front of the train that had brought Longarm, black smoke jetting from its diamond-shaped brass stack, two men in rugged trail garb stepped onto the passenger car's front vestibule. They pulled an iron ramp out from under the vestibule, and slid it smoothly and neatly down the top of the three steps to the ground.

Next they helped a man in a wheelchair out of the car's front door. One scurried to the bottom of the ramp while the other lowered him slowly, carefully down the ramp, pushing down on the chair's back handles to lift the front wheels a few inches off the ramp's corrugated iron surface.

Longarm continued to puff his own stogie as the tallest of the two ranch hands pushed the man toward the federal and the three waiting boosters, while the other ranch hand remained by the car, digging a hide tobacco sack from a shirt pocket.

The man in the squawky wooden wheelchair was a big, red-faced gent in a bowler hat and a charcoal gray serge suit. His shoulders were broad, his belly large, round, and hard behind a gray vest and a crisp white shirt and a bolo tie with a large stone. The tie's horsehair strings flapped over his shoulder in the hot breeze. All in all, he had a tough, rumpled, weathered look, wavy silver hair showing beneath the brim of his battered ancient Texas-creased Stetson.

Bart Spicer, manager of the Tres Pinos, grinned ruefully, lifting half of his upper lip above his large yellow front teeth as he approached Longarm and the others.

"Well, fuck me runnin'," he said as the tall, bandy-legged drover in a sugarloaf sombrero brought him to a stop in front of Longarm. "It's sure enough Deputy U.S. Marshal Custis P. Long. I knew Billy'd tried to send me the best hoss in his remuda, but I figured you'd be busy and I'd have to settle for some sissy counterfeit. Especially since we're dealin' with women, an' all. Most folks outside of us who've had run-ins with them four bitches with cougar jaws for pussies thinks this is all just a West Texas sham, and we're all sufferin' from heat stroke out here." He grinned fully now. "Or our mamas whipped us with ocotillo switches too damn much."

He'd been shaking Longarm's hand through most of that, and the big lawman thought he might have cracked a knuckle or two with his bear trap grip.

"Well, I can't comment on how your mothers treated you fellers when you were in swaddling clothes," Longarm said, picking up his warbag, which he'd dropped to shake the big, wheelchair-bound man's meaty paw, "but I can tell you I'll make every effort to run these gals to ground." He glanced at the three-combination train that looked like a toy nose up to the other, full-size one still spitting smoke and steam. "Handy little travelin' digs you have there, Mr. Spicer."

"The mucky-mucks over in England gave me that to travel around the great state of Texas in, to make the deals I got damn good at making and was still making . . . till cattle prices dropped and the fucking railroads started overcharging for shipping. Now I reckon it's mine since none o' them Limeys wants to travel this far to take it away. And how would they get it over the Atlantic anyway?"

Spicer laughed, grinning up at Longarm.

"Call me Bart."

"Then call me Longarm."

"I was hopin' I could!"

"Shall we head on over to the hotel, gentlemen?" said Pringle, gesturing with a long-fingered, beringed hand. "I have a table waiting."

"Fine as frog hair," said Spicer, glancing back and up at the rangy Texan piloting his wheelchair, who then pushed him forward along the deep, well-churned dust and shit of the street.

They crossed a bridge over a narrow stream and along which cottonwoods and Manzanita grass grew. There wasn't much water in the cut, but Longarm suspected it was still a healthy stream for dry West Texas in mid to late summer. It probably made growing hay possible on the large and small spreads that likely surrounded the town and populated the valley.

As Longarm strolled along with the group, he saw several ramps angling down from boardwalks fronting several establishments up and down the street. Something told him these were for the Tres Pinos manager, likely denoting the places he frequented most when he charmed Santa Clara with a visit.

They also told how much financial weight he pulled around here. Most of the wooden ramps, the federal lawman noted, angled down from boardwalks fronting saloons, with another servicing the Santa Clara Cattleman's Association and another angling along the steps of the gaudy three-story, balconied hotel they were now approaching—the Guadalupe House hotel and saloon.

"That south side could use another coat of paint, Pringle," Spicer told the hotel owner, whose cheeks flushed instantly, his shoulders tightening slightly at the Tres Pinos manager's gall. "Wanna keep ole Santa Clara lookin' like the white folks moved in, now, don't we? Not like the Mescins still run things."

He chuckled as the rangy ranch hand pulled him up the hotel ramp backward, and the others waited at the top of the steps, Pringle's cheeks dimpling with silent anger.

When they were all seated in the hotel's plush dining room outfitted with a deep plush purple and burgundy carpet, potted palms, decorative mirrors, crystal chandeliers, and round tables adorned with white cloth, glistening silverware, and crisp white china, Pringle asked a waiter to bring them drinks. The waiter did not actually serve the drinks, however. A woman did. A tooth-grindingly beautiful brunette with hazel eyes and a gold locket studded with a single turquoise bead dangling down across a rich, inviting bosom all but revealed by her frilly, low-cut, cream-colored gown.

"Good afternoon, gentlemen," the woman said, instantly locking gazes with Longarm. "I thought I'd bring the drinks out and have my husband introduce me to the new lawman in town."

Pringle hesitated, shifting his obviously nervous glance between Longarm and the delightful creature passing around the beer, cognac, and whiskies, her corset nearly spilling every ounce of its delightful, creamy contents onto the table before the gaping men. "Uh . . . yes, of course. Deputy Long, this is my dear wife, Matilda. She runs the hotel desk and the kitchen. Matilda, dear—this is Deputy Long from Denver, here to bridle those savage she-cats I'm sure you've heard about."

Longarm's tongue had dried to a flap of sun-wizened

leather. Awkwardly, he rose, stumbling a little and shoving out his hand. "Pleased as punch to meet you, Mrs. Pringle. Call me Longarm."

"The pleasure is all mine," Matilda Pringle said raspily, sexily, giving Longarm's hand a slight squeeze and demurely lowering her lids over her mesmerizing hazel eyes. Glancing at her husband but continuing to hold Longarm's hand in hers, she added, "And yes, I have heard of those she-cats. Just awful, aren't they? Oh, what's the world coming to, Marshal Long?"

Chapter 7

Matilda Pringle gave Longarm's hand one more gentle squeeze then released it.

"I ask myself the same question eight or nine times a day, Mrs. Pringle." Longarm gave the hazel-eyed brunette a winning smile, aware of her husband watching them both with narrow-eyed concern. "Rest assured, however, that the trouble here will soon be over."

"Oh?" Mrs. Pringle cocked a brow. "Do you think you alone can take down this gang of formidable cutthroats, who've stolen so much, killed so many, and"— she glanced at the banker—"pulled that awful stunt on Mr. Whitehurst?"

A crimson blush rose behind the banker's sunburn, and he dropped his broad, red-whiskered face in apparent chagrin.

"Oh?" Longarm said, raking his gaze from the beauty to the four other men seated around the table. "What awful stunt was that?"

"We'll get to that, Deputy Long," said Mr. Pringle.

"All in due time. Matilda, dear, don't you think you'd better check the kitchen?" He arched his sandy brows, lines of reproof cutting across his forehead and badly receding hairline. "And since the stage is due in a few minutes, you'll need to take over the hotel desk."

The hazel-eyed beauty lifted the drink tray off the table and lowered her chin demurely to her husband. "Of course, Madison." A faint note of sarcasm entered her voice as she glanced at the banker. "And I do apologize if I was speaking out of turn, Mr. Whitehurst. It's just that I thought since everyone in town saw what happened—"

"That will be enough, Matilda—thank you!" cajoled her husband.

She smiled at Longarm. "Nice meeting you, uh, Longarm." Her brows beetled slightly, curiously. Longarm . . . what a strange name. Well, I wish you luck!" As she backed away from the table, the locket bounced across her high, uptilted bosom, which the brawny federal lawman was having trouble keeping his eyes off of. There was a very tiny mole, he noticed, about two inches down from the top of her cleavage and on the inside of her left breast. God, what he wouldn't give to run his tongue across it . . .

Realizing he'd let his gaze stray once more, he lifted it back to the woman's face. She'd had her eyes on his, so obviously she'd known exactly what they'd been drawn to. Without letting on, however—unless holding his gaze for just a stretched half-second was letting on— she turned and walked away with the tray toward the kitchen doors at the back of the room. Her rump swayed deliciously inside the dress that fit her form wonderfully.

Her rich, chestnut locks cascaded down her slender back and narrow shoulders.

She was gone, but her womanly smell lingered.

"Lovely young lady," Longarm said, noticing that all eyes were on him. Spicer's, Whitehurst's, and Braun's were vaguely complicitous, as though they were fully aware of the woman's beauty. The girl's husband's brow-arched gaze, however, showed disapproval at the attention Longarm couldn't help but show the man's wife.

"Yes, she is beautiful, and I do love Matilda dearly," said Pringle, raising his cognac glass to his lips capped with a carefully trimmed, silver-gray mustache, "and I guess I can't blame her for being a bit of a chatterbox. She works quite hard around here—owning a hotel is not for the meek, I assure you—and being the loquacious sort, she does enjoy a spell of rest and conversation now and then. Fortunately, I've introduced her to a nice set of ladies who regularly attend our church."

"You know who you can thank for Matilda, eh, Pringle?" Bart Spicer raised his whiskey shot in salute, and gave the hotel owner a wink before throwing back half the hooch and splashing the rest into his beer, chuckling.

Longarm was hoping the ranch manager's comment might be explained, but it served only to make Pringle look even more uncomfortable, smoothing his mustache and goatee as he glanced over at Whitehurst, who still looked a little flustered by Matilda's comment regarding him.

"I do apologize for my wife's remarks, Angus."

"Quite all right," said Whitehurst, an English lilt to his voice. "I imagine most people in town do know of that rather humbling experience. I can only hope the four young ladies who attacked on me will be all the more humbled."

"I'd like to break in here," Longarm said, growing annoyed, "and ask what in hell happened out there. I'm sorry for your embarrassment, Whitehurst, but I need to know everything, and the sooner I do, the sooner I can get after those four she-cats."

The rancher snorted and dropped his gaze to his whiskey-laced beer. Pringle and Braun both looked sympathetic.

Whitehurst, with true English aplomb, lifted his dimbled, flame-shaped chin resolutely, tugged on one bushy red muttonchop, and said as though to an invisible presence somewhere over Longarm's right shoulder, "Once a month, I transport the payroll money out to the Chainlink Ranch. Norman Vance, the owner and operator of the ranch—not a large spread at all, employing only ten or twelve men—and myself are good friends. He has family back in England, as I do. I like to ride out, have drinks and dinner with Mr. Vance and his wife, Norma, and spend the night in their guest cottage. I usually ride in my surrey with two men riding guard.

"Well, last week I rode out with my two guards. We were riding up near Kiowa Butte when both guards were summarily shot out of their saddles. Of course, I thought I was next. I waited, unarmed, clutching the Chainlink's payroll to my breast, expecting a bullet at any time. None came. Who did come were the four lovely hell riders in question here. They did not kill me, and I suppose for that I can be grateful. However, they took the money from me, ordered me to strip naked at gunpoint . . ."

Whitehurst let his voice trail off to glare at Spicer,

who'd given another snort as he stared down at his beer glass.

"Oh, come on, Angus . . ." The ranch manager beseeched the man's understanding, chuckling then taking a long drink from his beer to cover his obvious amusement.

Whitehurst blinked and turned his gaze back to the invisible presence flanking Longarm.

"As I was saying, those lovely demons found great joy in ordering me to strip down to my absolute birthday suit, without even a hat to protect me from the harsh desert sun, or socks to cushion my feet from cactus thorns, and sending me back to Santa Clara, blowing up dust all around me with their revolvers."

Whitehurst continued to stare past Longarm as an uncomfortable silence fell over the table.

Spicer fidgeted then glanced at the banker. "You shouldn't go anywhere unarmed, Angus. Not even when you got armed men with you. This is Texas, fer Chrissakes. *West* Texas."

"You know Angus doesn't know how to shoot," said Mayor Braun scoldingly, his eye monocle flashing in the light from one of the tall front windows. "Besides, if his armed riders were defenseless against those women, how could he fare any better if armed with a Peacemaker?"

"You must have gotten a good look at 'em," Longarm told the banker. "Did you recognize 'em?"

Whitehurst looked confused by the question. "Yes, I suppose I did see them . . . but . . . for the life of me I couldn't describe them . . . beyond telling you that all four were . . . *beautiful*!" His brows mantled his eyes as he looked down at his hands on the table, on either side of his brandy snifter.

"How much they get?" Longarm asked the obviously chagrined banker.

"Four thousand, five hundred dollars. Not much considering what they took from the Army payroll a few days later."

"Army payroll?"

Whitehurst explained that five Army payroll riders from Fort Comanche had been killed, as well as three other men, and that twenty-six thousand dollars had been looted from the strongbox. Spicer's own riders had come upon the scene's aftermath in the bloody canyon, and found four sets of woman-sized boot prints near the dead men, and four sets of shod hoofprints all clustered together where the women had likely tied the mounts when they'd staged their ambush. The sheriff over in Juniper had been sent a telegraph, as had the commanding officer at Fort Comanche, but neither man had as yet been seen.

It was a big country, Spicer assured Longarm. And when the country didn't almost literally swallow folks up, it took them a long, hard time getting anywhere.

"You sure it was these killer women?" Longarm asked.

"The smaller boot prints—four sets—tell the story. Too much of a coincidence for it to be another four riders with small feet, if you ask me."

"Billy Vail told me you got a personal stake in this," Longarm told the ranch manager.

"Sure as hell do," Spicer said, setting his beer in both his big, leathery hands. "A big one."

He sat back in his wheelchair, glowering across the table at Longarm. If he felt uncomfortable sitting about two inches lower than the others, he didn't show it. His frame was formidable even in the wheelchair, his face large and raw as sun-blasted granite, his silver hair thick and wavy. His hat was resting on a chair near the rangy gent who'd wheeled him into the hotel dining room and who was now waiting out in the lobby; it wasn't his station to dine with Spicer and Santa Clara mucky-mucks.

"Them bitches killed my segundo, Red Hollinbach, about a month ago. Red came down from Montana by special invitation from me when I took over the Tres Pinos. A good man. Now he's dead, and I don't know where in the hell I'll find another one like Red."

"You said three men were killed."

"Giff Clawson and Billy Honeycutt. It was their day off, and they were hoisting a few at the Massacre Creek Saloon. Them women came in like it was their duty to kill those boys, and that's exactly what they done. Only, like what they done to Whitehurst, they humiliated 'em first."

Longarm was about to ask for more details regarding the humiliation, but Spicer jumped in as though to get it over with. "Made 'em take their peckers out. That clear enough for you?"

Pringle cleared his throat behind his fist. The other two men looked a little glass-eyed.

Longarm blinked, not sure he'd heard the man correctly. "Any particular reason they made 'em take their peckers out?"

"To humiliate 'em, same as they did to—"

"Oh, come on, now, Spicer," Pringle put in. "You know that is not the full story. Whip Freeman . . ." The hotel owner glanced at Longarm. "Freeman's the proprietor of the Massacre Creek Saloon." Turning back to Spicer, he said, "Freeman said it seemed as though the women were getting back at your men for a, uh, recent *indiscretion*."

Longarm waited.

Another heavy silence settled over the table until Pringle turned to Longarm. "The four pistoleras accused Mr. Spicer's boys, Hollinbach included, of raping a young girl from Crossfire Valley."

"Red wouldn't have done that!" Spicer pointed an angry finger across the table at Pringle. "I don't know about Honeycutt and Clawson, they only been on the roll a few months, but Red never woulda taken no girl unwilling-like. If that girl was raped, she did somethin' to instigate it." He laughed caustically. "And I think it highly unlikely it could honestly be called rape! She was one o' them Crossfire Girls, after all!"

"Easy, Bart," Pringle warned.

Spicer gave a chuff and sat back in his chair once more, brushing a fist across his mouth and looking away from the table in silent defiance.

Longarm looked around the table, all the men around him now looking both angry and chagrined for their own private reasons. "Look, gentlemen," Longarm said with an ironic snort, "I feel like I'm drownin' in quicksand here, and the sand keeps getting deeper and deeper. Who's the girl from Crossfire Valley, and where in the hell *is* Crossfire Valley? Oh, and before I forget, I'm gonna need to know how I can get ahold of this Whip Freeman from Massacre Creek! I have a couple more needling points to consider, but let's start with those two for now. Once I get those answers, I'm sure I'll have more ques . . ."

Longarm let his voice trail off. He'd just seen a vaguely familiar figure pass outside a window in the saloon's front wall, partly obscured by drawn curtains but familiar just the same. Something about the hunch of his shoulders and the choppy way he walked . . .

Pringle looked at Longarm, as did the other men, frowning curiously. "Yes? What is it, Deputy Long?"

Longarm sat tensely. Boot thuds sounded in the lobby, and then the man he'd seen pass in front of the hotel walked in his choppy gait into the dining room. He wore a long, black, dusty coat, and a black opera hat. He had a long, horsey face, and on his thimble-sized wreck of a nose perched a pair of round, iron-rimmed spectacles.

He made a beeline for the table at which Longarm sat with Spicer and the other Santa Clara town councilmen, and the bizarre smile that suddenly stretched across his face made Longarm begin to think he might be a long-lost acquaintance.

The man long-strode up to the table, and stopped, his fishy blue eyes looking extra large behind the grime-smeared thick lenses of his glasses. "Deputy United States Marshal Custis Long?"

Under the table, Longarm had snaked his right hand across his belly and released the keeper thong from over his Colt's hammer. "Who's askin'?"

"Grogan Caulfield, Longarm. Got a message for you from the Four Horsewomen of the Apocalypse."

The man swept a flap of his black frock coat back from his hip and, howling like a maniac, raised a sawed-off, double-barreled shotgun.

Chapter 8

"Down!" Longarm shouted as he triggered his double-action six-shooter beneath the table.

Blam-blam-blam!

His shots were slightly muffled beneath the table, from where he'd taken hasty aim while trying to shoot between Bart Spicer and Angus Whitehurst. Before his last shot had finished resounding, the shotgunner's victorious howl turned to a scream. His shotgun drooped slightly.

Ka-boooom!

Both barrels sprouted roses, hammering the middle of the white-clothed table with double-ought buckshot at close range. Two pumpkin-sized craters were blown into the table, spitting burning cloth and wood slivers in all directions.

At the same time, the tall, black-clad shooter screamed and twisted around and stumbled backward, telling Longarm that at least one of his lugs had drilled one or both of the man's legs. Longarm lunged to his feet, throwing his own chair back behind him, and taking aim at the black-clad man once more. The man fell hard on the saloon floor and was still screaming as he brought up a pearl-gripped Colt from a shoulder holster under his left arm.

"Hold it!" Longarm shouted, wanting the man alive.

"Hold this, Longarm!" the man wailed, bringing the big black Colt up but swinging it around uncertainly, again threatening the lives of the men around Longarm, two of whom had hit the floor while Spicer dropped his big, gray head to the table and covered it with his thick arms.

Longarm's own Colt leaped twice more in his fist, spitting smoke and flames. The slugs punched through the ambusher's chest about six inches apart, slamming him straight back onto the floor. He made a strangling sound, eyes bulging, blood pumping thickly from the wounds. He fell still, his cocked Colt lying on the carpeted floor nearby.

As Longarm stepped around the table, he spied movement to his left, and swung his Colt in that direction. It was Matilda Pringle. She'd just stepped out of the kitchen door, eyes wide in shock and fear at the explosions. Now she gasped as she stared at Longarm's Colt bearing down on her. He lowered the weapon with a relieved sigh—no telling how many bushwhackers were after him—and continued around the table to the man he'd shot.

"Good Christ!" exclaimed Bart Spicer, who'd lifted his head from the table to stare down at the dead man. "Well, you drilled the bastard good—I'll give you that, Longarm. Seen you do it in the street in Abilene." He turned to Whitehurst and Braun, both of whom had thrown themselves to the floor and were now slowly, cautiously climbing back to their feet. "Didn't I tell you this was the only law-bringin' hombre for the job?"

Longarm didn't need to inspect the dead man very carefully to know he was a goner. Both his bullets had shredded the fool's black heart, and now all his blood was leaking out onto the deep, plush carpet.

"Grogan Caulfield," he muttered, studying the man's slack-featured face, his glasses hanging askew. "Sure as hell," he muttered. "Indian agent from—"

"Madison!"

Longarm turned to see Matilda Pringle crouching down on the other side of the table, behind the empty chair of her husband.

Braun looked down to his left, and exclaimed, "Pringle!"

Longarm hurried around Spicer to the other side of the table and saw the hotel owner lying propped on his arm and looking miserable, feebly trying to rise though his left arm was oozing blood from a dozen or so small buckshot wounds not only in his arm but in his shoulder, as well.

Both Braun and Matilda knelt down beside the wounded hotel owner, who grunted and groaned as he glanced down at the dribbling blood. "Oh, good Lord," Pringle moaned, his features bleaching as he saw the shape he was in. "Oh, mercy—I've . . . I've been shot. Oh, good Lord!"

"It's not that bad, Madison," said Mrs. Pringle, jerking her head around to the rangy cowboy who'd accompanied Spicer and was now standing protectively near his boss, holding a Schofield pistol down low at his side. He looked as shocked as all the others. "Vernon, fetch Doc MacLeish—*quick*!"

Vernon looked dumbly down at his boss. "That what you want me to do, Mr. Spicer?"

"Do as the lady says, Vernon. I'm fine. Be quick about it, for cryin' out loud!"

When Vernon had gone, Longarm holstered his pistol and nudged Mrs. Pringle aside, snaking one arm under Pringle's wounded left shoulder. "Let's get you to your feet, Pringle. Get you into a chair and see just how bad this is."

"Oh, Lord," Pringle said. "I've never been shot before."

"I think your wife's on the mark here, Pringle."

Longarm eased the man into his chair, crouched over him, and ripped his shirt open with both hands, sending buttons flying and his string tie flopping down on his naked chest. He kept tearing the shirt until he'd gotten it down off his shoulder. He gave it another hard jerk, and the entire sleeve, splitting at the seam, fell away from his arm.

Pringle's eyes widened at the blood oozing from the small wounds. "Oh, Lord!" He sagged against Longarm, who caught the man, and eased him back in his chair.

"Is he dead?" asked Braun, himself nearly undone by the sudden violence and the wounding of the hotelier.

"Nah, nah," Longarm chuckled. "Some folks handle the sight of blood a little better than other folks."

He glanced at the man's wife, who raised her eyebrows. "He has a fit if he cuts himself shaving." She looked at the table with the giant hole in the middle, and the dead man on the floor. "Good Lord," she whispered.

"Someone better fetch the marshal," said Braun, glancing from Pringle to the table to the dead man.

"You're forgettin'," Spicer said, wheeling his chair back from the table and producing a fat cigar from his shirt pocket. "Them fuckin' bitches—uh, pardon my French, Mrs. Pringle—done gave old Arden Anderson a pill he couldn't digest, and the menfolk ain't exactly been clamorin' for the job with these pistol-wieldin' ladies on the loose."

He looked at Longarm, who'd turned the wounded hotelier over to his wife and walked over to one of the front windows, casting wary glances up and down the street. "You know this hombre, Longarm? He sure seemed to know you."

"Grogan Caulfield, just like he said. Was an Injun agent up in Dakota Territory, before I run him to ground for sellin' Injun girls and boys to slave traders. Don't know how he got out of prison, but he did, sure enough, and how he knew I was here, when I just done *got* here, I got no idea."

"Maybe he just spied you on the street and decided to get even right here and now," said Whitehurst, who was standing back a ways from the table, as though afraid more violence was imminent.

Sweat streaked his cheeks, dampening his curly red muttonchops.

"Good Lord—I hope there aren't more where he came from!"

"Mr. Longarm," said the monocled Mayor Braun, holding his brandy in a shaky hand as he stood beside the passed-out hotelier and Mrs. Pringle, "no offense or anything, but I'd just as soon not be in the same room with you anymore, while you're here. A man like your-

self obviously packs a few enemies, including the Four
Horsewomen of the Apocalypse themselves!"

With that, Braun threw back his drink, picked up
his hat from the table—it, too, wore several small buckshot holes—and long-strode through the dining room
door and into the lobby, gone.

Longarm glanced at the others in the room, including
Mrs. Pringle, regarding him like some old cur with the
mange, then gave a sardonic chuff as he continued gaz-
ing out the window, his glance catching on the waiting
gallows.

Around ten o'clock the next morning, Longarm pulled
his hat brim low against the climbing sun and halted his
rented buckskin on the bank of Bayonet Wash. On the
opposite bank were eight separate graves—mounded dirt
covered with rocks and fronted by a single large cross
constructed of two ironwood branches and a cut length
of a puncher's woven riata.

Likely, Spicer's men, who'd found the bodies of the
soldiers and the three civilians, had done the burying.
There was a dead horse on the wash's sandy floor, half-
eaten by scavengers and sending up a heavy fetor. Longarm would have liked a look at the three dead civilians,
but he'd be damned if he'd dig up the two-week-old
carcasses.

Puzzling, though—five dead Army payroll riders and
three civilians. Had the civilians been riding with the
soldiers?

He looked around, his gaze falling on something
shiny in the rocks on his side of the wash. Swinging his
right leg over his saddle horn, he dropped to the ground
flat-footed, and walked into the rocks on the lip of the

steep ridge. He squatted on his heels, picked up one of the several .44-40 cartridge casings that littered the area.

A minute later he scrambled on down the bank, noticing three sets of faint boot tracks scarring the slanting game trail. A slow, thorough perusal of the area gave him a few of the answers to the questions needling him.

The three civilians had apparently ambushed the caravan from the western ridge, leaving their casings to tell their story. Around the strongbox that remained near the dead, bloated horse carcass were more boot prints and a lot of blood that had turned a flaky brown against the orange sand and gravel. Man-sized boot prints. One definitely matched one of those from the side of the ridge.

That meant the civilians had been going through the money when they'd been killed, shot from down canyon a ways, where several sets of revolver casings were strewn amid the sand, gravel, and prickly pear. Those tracks had faded over the past several days, leaving Longarm to take the word of Spicer's men.

They'd been left by the Four Horsewomen of the Apocalypse, as the kill-crazy young maidens seemed to want to be known.

Longarm walked a ways down canyon, and downwind from the stench of the dead horse, and lowered the bandanna he'd covered his nose and mouth with. He sat down in the shade of the wash's eastern ridge, dug a three-for-a-nickel cheroot from his shirt pocket, and scraped a stove match to life on his thumbnail.

He drew a deep lungful of the pleasingly pungent tobacco smoke, held it for a pensive few seconds before blowing it out. Nothing like smoking a cheap cigar to soothe the soul, ease the old thinker box, and help the thoughts along . . .

Who were these gals and what compelled them?
Were they out for revenge or just money? Or both? Obviously, they aimed to terrorize.

Why?

What about the girl from the Crossfire Valley? Longarm would like to find her though none of the men in
town could remember her name or where she lived, just
that she came from the valley. If the four deadly horsewomen had shot Spicer's men to avenge this girl, then
this girl likely knew them and might be able to tell Longarm where he'd find them. Otherwise, since no one else
seemed able to identify them, he was for all intents and
purposes chasing specters around these hills.

He flicked ashes off his cigar and thought of the man
called Freeman who ran the saloon at Massacre Creek.
He'd witnessed the murder of Spicer's men. Maybe he
could give Longarm some clue as to the deadly horsewomen's identities. Longarm had had Spicer draw him a
rough map of the area, and having inspected it closely
last night before turning into the bed of his rented room
at the Pringles' hotel, he knew generally where he could
find Massacre Creek from here.

Rising with a grunt and taking another deep drag
from his cigar, he climbed the eastern bank and stared
toward a low jog of tan hills to the northeast. At the base
of those hills, according to Spicer's map, lay the twisting
course of Massacre Creek, so named after a long-ago
war between the Kiowa and the Apache.

A few minutes later, he'd mounted his buckskin and
was heading toward the hills at a horse-saving trot. Al-
ternating trots and lopes and stopping once to water both
himself and the horse at a muddy spring, he gained the
roadhouse flanking a railroad bed an hour later.

As he rode into the yard of the long, low-slung, mud-and-log, brush-roofed cabin, he saw something move in the open door. He jerked back on the buckskin's reins as smoke puffed in the doorway.

At the same time that dust kicked up just right of his gelding's front hooves, the clap of the rifle reached Longarm's ears. His Frontier Model Colt was in his hand before he knew it. He aimed and fired, saw a shabby green hat blow off a man's large head low on the doorway's right side.

The man in the doorway screamed and stumbled back into the cabin and out of sight.

Longarm cursed. Hurling himself from his saddle, he dropped the buckskin's reins and ran toward the cabin.

Chapter 9

Longarm mounted the gallery in one leap and swung right of the door, which was propped open by a rock. He pressed his back to the log front wall and turned his head toward the opening, beyond which he could hear grunting and the thuds of someone crawling along the wooden floor.

He glanced inside, seeing no one near the front door, so he bolted through the opening and stepped to his left, putting his back to the wall, his index finger drawing taut against the .44's trigger. As his eyes adjusted to the dingy shadows, he saw a man crawling along the bar on the room's right side, heading for the other end.

Longarm drilled two slugs into the bar over the man's nearly bald head, and he dropped to the floor, covering his head with his pale, meaty arms.

"Why'n the hell you tryin' to perforate me, amigo?" Holding his gun on the man on the floor, Longarm raked his gaze across the saloon—a long, low hall with about seven tables and an iron heating stove. Beyond was a closed door to the outside. The man on the floor appeared to be alone here.

Not far from Longarm, the rifle the man had used to snap a shot at him lay beneath a table.

"Lessen the custom's different here in Texas, it ain't no way to greet prospective customers."

Longarm lowered his pistol and walked along the bar, his low-heeled cavalry boots thudding loudly. The man lowered an arm and turned his head toward him. The dark brown eyes set beneath gray-flecked brown brows dropped to the copper moon-and-star marshal's badge pinned to Longarm's vest, beneath the lapel of his black frock coat.

"Ah, shit," the man said, breathless. "You a lawman?"

"If you'd have let me get a little closer before you tried boring a hole in my head, you might have seen the badge."

The man—big and round, with a bullet-shaped head crowned with thin, sweaty, curly gray-brown hair—lowered his other arm and rose onto a shoulder. He ran his arm across his sweaty face, blinking and shaking his head. "I do apologize, friend. I seen ya comin', an' it's been so awful quiet out here, I thought I seen long hair bobbin' around your shoulders, and I sorta threw a kingbolt. Grabbed my Spencer there . . . oh, shit—I need a drink."

With a grunt, he gained his feet and ambled to a near table on which a bottle and a dirty glass sat along with an open illustrated *Policeman's Gazette* and an ashtray in which a cornhusk quirley smoldered.

"Looks like you mighta had enough to drink."

"Can I offer you one?" The man held up the bottle.

"Got any Maryland rye?"

The drink-rheumy eyes narrowed. "What kinda rye?"

"I'll take a beer."

The man took a long pull from his bottle, puffed his cigarette, returned it to the ashtray, then ambled breathlessly around behind the bar.

Longarm holstered his Colt and propped a foot on a chair. "You Whip Freeman?"

The barman looked over the spigot handle beneath which he was holding a beer schooner. "That's right. You're here about them women, ain't ya? 'Bout time someone does somethin' about those evil witches. I thought the Army would send somebody around after the ambush in Bayonet Wash, but . . ."

He set the filled schooner, topped with an inch of creamy foam, onto the counter, and nodded at it. "That there's free. Any customer I try to drill due to a bad case of the fantods gets a free beer." He backed up a step and ran his hands up and down on his apron, chuckling nervously.

"Jake of ya." Longarm walked over and picked up the beer. "I just came from the wash."

"Any sign of them women yet?"

"Not yet. That's why I rode here." Longarm sipped the beer, surprised to find it not only hefty and malty, but not altogether bad despite being warm. Freeman was probably German—lots of Germans in Texas, and they were damn good beer makers.

Licking foam from his mustached upper lip, he looked down at the floor. He'd seen the broad bloodstain when he'd tramped along the bar after the barman. Now he inspected it, saw the deep brown crust wedged between the floorboards and embedded in the cracks.

"That's what they left of Red, Giff, and Billy," the

barman said, walking out from behind the bar again, heading for his table with an eager eye on his bottle. "Them women done humiliated 'em good then shot all three and piled 'em up cold with their peckers hangin' out."

"Could you describe 'em to me?"

The barman turned to Longarm, eyes thoughtful, befuddled.

"Never mind. Did you see which way they headed when they left here after killing the Tres Pinos boys?"

"Hell, no. I was too busy pukin' my guts up after I seen their handiwork."

Longarm looked at his beer in frustration. "The girls said the reason they shot those fellas was because of a girl from Crossfire Valley." Longarm took another sip of his beer and put his back to the bar, facing the barman, who sagged down in a creaky chair before his bottle and open magazine. "You know the name?"

"Never heard of it before them witches mentioned it." Freeman splashed whiskey into his glass, filling it one-quarter full. He stared down at it, considering, then poured another couple of fingers. "Think it mighta been Angie."

"They said those men raped that girl."

"I know—I was here, remember? But I don't know no Angie. Probably some jackleg rancher's daughter. Maybe from over in Crossfire Valley." He chuffed his disdain at the name.

Longarm pondered the name *Crossfire Valley* again. If he didn't run the four killers to ground soon, he'd be paying a visit there.

"Where is this place?"

"Northwest. Borders the Tres Pinos range. In fact,

they diverted Crossfire Creek away from it about two years ago. Left them settlers high an' dry. Nothin' but a bunch o' Scotch-Irish and Mescins anyway."

"What's so bad about the Scotch-Irish and Mescins?"

"What's good about 'em?" Freeman killed half his drink in two swallows then ran a fat hand across his mouth. "Besides, their women are whores. Everyone knows that. That Angie girl likely had it comin'. Prob'ly a cock-teaser." He took a deep puff off his quirley, ashes dropping from the long coal and onto the magazine on the table. "Red, Giff, and Billy were regular customers. And I don't have many customers of any stripe—regular or otherwise—no more!"

"Sorry to hear that."

Longarm kicked out a chair and sat down. Well, he'd learned the general location of Crossfire Valley if nothing else, anyway. As it was on the other side of Santa Clara, he'd have to save it for another day. It was already noon, and by the time he got back to town, if he left now, it would be too late, and besides, he and the buckskin would be blown.

And he wanted to ride around a bit first, see if he happened to break the sign of the four riders. It would be sheer luck if he did. But sometimes all a lawman had to rely on was his luck, and Longarm felt damn lucky to have survived the job as long as he had.

"Well, I'll be moseyin'," he told Freeman when he'd finished his beer. Heading to the door and donning his hat, he said without turning his head to the barman, "If you remember anything about those four, anything at all, you get word to me in Santa Clara. I'm holed up at the Guadalupe House."

"Watch your back, lawman."

As Longarm stepped through the door, he stopped and looked behind now at Freeman, who was shooting him a fearful look, the loosely rolled quirley smoldering in a corner of his mouth. "I ain't sure they're human. They're purty as border collie pups. But I ain't sure they ain't been sent straight from hell to kill every male in Guadalupe County!"

Longarm considered the man's words. "Ah, you're just superstitious, Freeman."

He tramped off the gallery and into the yard, gathered the buckskin's reins, and rode north along a faint horse trail winding through the tan hump of bald hills he didn't know the names of. But they looked like a good place for the kill-hungry she-cats to disappear into after they'd killed the Tres Pinos riders.

The landscape was decidedly moony out here.

It was all low bluffs and sand-colored cliffs and rocky, broken barrancas, with deep canyons at nearly every turn, craggy washes at other turns. It was easy to get turned around when the sun wasn't visible, and several times the federal lawman, who prided himself on his sense of direction, got turned around.

The sun got him headed back on a generally westward course.

He'd only been out here an hour when he started to think he was wasting his time and energy. He saw very little sign of anything except bobcats, mountain lions, wolves, coyotes, and occasional bears, let alone four horsewomen. He found a few horse apples, but none was under two weeks old. They probably belonged to the horses of ranch riders out looking for herd quitters or strays.

He doubted the women were out here. If they were, they kept themselves better hid than the bobcats did.

It was damn hot, as it generally was in West Texas in August. The heat blasted at him not only from out of the sky, but from off the rocks around him, as well. The few times he dismounted the buckskin, he could feel the heat searing the bottoms of his boots through the dirt.

Traversing a broad canyon, he was happy when he came upon three scraggly willows leaning near a trickling spring. Dismounting, he loosened the buckskin's saddle cinch and slipped the horse's bit from its teeth, so it could drink freely and rest. Longarm dropped down to the small bowl in the rocks, which was being filled one or two drops at a time from the spring in the shale a couple of feet above.

He'd touched his tongue to the tepid but still refreshing pool, when chicken flesh rose across the back of his neck. He lifted his head suddenly, water dribbling off his chin. His keen sixth sense had saved his life enough times that he'd learned not to ignore it.

Slowly, he straightened his back and rocked back on his heels, looking around at the rocky knobs on all sides of him, the sun-blasted slopes where the sun lay like a palpable presence and the cicadas sang their monotonous dirge. It was two or three in the afternoon, the westering sun sliding just enough shadows out from the boulders and cactus and sotol that a bushwhacker could conceal himself—or herself—relatively easily.

Again moving slowly, Longarm rose to a crouch and slid his Winchester from the buckskin's saddle sheath. In his vision's periphery, something moved, and he found himself diving forward as a slug spanged raucously off a rock just above the spring. The crack of the rifle in the rocks of a northern bluff sounded a half-second later.

Knowing he made a nice target down here, Longarm sprang off his hands and knees and bolted forward, sprinting, heading for a low rock shelf about twenty feet left of the spring. The rifle above kicked up dust at his boots, one nicking the edge of his heal enough that he could feel its nudge, causing the chicken flesh to sprout full flower.

He hunched beneath the shelf, racking a live cartridge into his Winchester's breech.

Another shot blasted from the slope above him. The buckskin screamed and went down hard, blood pumping from the wound in the center of its forehead. Longarm gritted his teeth, lifted his head and rifle above the shelf, and fired in the general direction from which the shots had come.

Watching his own slugs merely puff rock dust, he cursed and pulled his head back down beneath the shelf as the shooter above opened up on him again—three quick shots drilling the top of the shelf and sending rocks and gravel flying, peppering the dirt just out from his crouched position.

Longarm looked around. He saw the dead horse, the blood pool growing in the gravel beneath its head.

He angrily racked a fresh round in his rifle's breech. "Why, you fuckin' bitch."

Chapter 10

Longarm showed just enough of his head to draw fire from behind a boulder about sixty yards above him. He pulled his head back quickly behind the low shelf, wincing and gritting his teeth as the bushwhacker's bullets ripped into the slope and the trail around him, spanging wickedly off rocks.

As he hunkered there, waiting for the shooting to stop, he kept the image of the shooter's nest clear in his mind's eye. When the shooting stopped, the echoes flatting out around the canyon, he jerked his head and rifle up once more, and bearing down on the boulder beside a bent fir tree, and the brown-hatted head poking around the boulder's left side, he fired three times quickly.

His first bullet slammed into the rock face just inches right of the bushwhacker's head, and he could tell by the way the shooter pulled his or her head back quickly, he'd likely peppered the bitch's face (who else would it be?) with sharp rock shards and maybe even some lead slivers from the slug.

He triggered three more rounds, then, knowing he had the shooter at bay, he scrambled quickly up the chalky, eroded slope above the shelf, heading for another shelf ten feet beyond. He'd make his way up the slope by small increments, picking his way from one cover to another until he'd gained the ambusher's nest, and blow the little bitch out of her hole.

When he gained the second shelf, he hunkered down again, poking his hat brim out just far enough to draw more shots. None came. There were only the cicadas and a light, vagrant breeze, the occasional rustling of the dry grass and agave that tufted out from between boulders.

Squeezing his rifle in both gloved hands, Longarm bolted out to the side of the shelf, bore down on the shooter's cover, and fired once to hold the shooter there. His bullet's ricochet off the boulder was still echoing as he bolted up the slope, heading for a rock eight feet above. In the upper periphery of his vision, he spied movement. He felt the tug on his left arm an eye blink before the echo's flat report reached his ears.

He groaned and stopped crawling up the slope just as another slug blew up sand and gravel six inches in front of his head. If he'd kept moving, he'd have had an extra hole in his head. As more slugs puffed dust around him, the ambusher's rifle thundering wickedly, he threw himself back down the slope and scrambled back behind the shelf he'd just left.

"Fuck!"

The curse was more from frustration than pain, because he could feel only a slight sting in his arm. When he looked down at it, he cursed again, more sharply, and clamped a hand over the blood welling up and glistening from the six-inch slit across his white shirtsleeve, halfway between his elbow and his shoulder.

He pulled his legs down behind the shelf as two more shots ripped into the gravel around his boots, and pressed his back against the slope, half-sitting but keeping his head down. The bitch could shoot—he'd give her that. Sounded like only one shooter, though. For that he was grateful. If all four of the Horsewomen of the Apocalypse could shoot as well as the one currently pinning him down, he'd be in a pickle.

He chuffed a dark laugh as he dug a bandanna out of his coat pocket and wrapped it around the bullet burn across his upper left arm. He was in a pickle the way it was. His would-be assassin had the high ground, and she wasn't missing her target, presumably Longarm's head, by much. He wondered how much ammo she had. He hoped less than he did.

He also wondered what she was doing out here. According to Spicer's map, he was currently on a corner of the massive holdings of Tres Pinos Ranch.

Running a couple of fingers across his cartridge belt, he counted eight more rifle shells. With the five shells in his Colt, leaving the chamber beneath the hammer empty so he wouldn't shoot himself in the leg, he had a total of ten for the handgun. He had a whole box in his saddlebags on the dead horse, but he'd never make it down to the horse without getting his head shot off.

He tightened the bandanna on his arm, wincing against the pain. The bullet had carved a nice trough across his

arm, but as long as he got the bleeding stopped, he'd
be all right. At the moment, he had larger things to
worry about.

He slipped cartridges from his shell belt, thumbing
them into the Winchester and keeping his ears pricked
for anyone trying to work around him. He was relatively
certain there was only one shooter, but he hadn't lived as
long as he had by taking chances.

And there were four women in the pack . . .

Gravel rattled from somewhere above. He froze, lis-
tening, holding a shell casing against the loading gate.

More gravel rattled, and then there were the larger
clatters of falling stones. Longarm shoved the cartridge
through the loading gate, racked a round into the chamber, and shoved his head out from behind the shelf, pulling it back quickly. No shot came. He edged his head
out once more, carefully, and peered up the rocky slope
toward the boulder.

Nothing there but the boulder itself. The slope rose
above it to a jagged crest. Behind the crest lay another,
higher bluff capped with more rocks and piñon pines
and flanked by the brassy Texas summer sky.

He looked to either side of the boulder the shooter
was—or had been—crouched behind. Nothing there but
more rock. He'd thought maybe she'd lit out to try and
slip around him, but he'd be damned if he saw anything
but sunblasted rock all around him. No more gravel fell.

Longarm waited, staying low, ready to raise the rifle
and start firing. The heat weighed on his shoulders, siz-
zled on the back of his neck, burned his left ear.

He spied movement at the crest of the ridge, and
jerked the rifle up. No . . . the movement wasn't on the
ridge directly above him, but on the next ridge over. A

horseback rider slanted up from behind the first ridge. The skewbald paint horse he or she was riding lunged off its back hooves, digging into the uncertain surface with its front hooves. The rider's back faced Longarm, and from this distance of several hundred yards he couldn't with any certainty make out the person's sex. Horse and rider were little larger than the lawman's thumb. The rider was wearing a tan hat and a tan duster, and light blond hair tumbled down his or her back—that was as much as he could tell. The blond hair meant the rider was likely female.

Horse and rider crested the ridge, galloped into the pines and boulders, and disappeared.

Longarm pulled his rifle down. She must have been getting toward the bottom of her shell supply. He took a long look around, making sure the shooter's fleeing wasn't a ploy to draw him out into the open, then slowly, he cautiously did just that. He walked down to the trail and scowled at the dead buckskin.

Another glance at the sky told him he had maybe four hours of light left. He wasn't sure how far he was from Santa Clara, but he'd never make it before sunset. Not afoot.

He inspected his arm. The bandanna was soaked with blood. He couldn't tell if the bleeding had stopped beneath the cloth. Didn't matter. He'd get a ways down the trail, set up camp in an hour or so or when he'd worn the soles out of his boots, and tend it then.

It took some work to get his saddlebags out from beneath the horse's dead weight, and he was glad to see the horse hadn't fallen on the pouch in which he kept his ubiquitous bottle of Maryland rye. He'd need the hooch for fortification later, and to clean the wound with.

He got his saddle and rifle scabbard off the dead horse, as well. Sweating like a butcher, the wound in his arm more irritating than anything, he dropped down to the spring for a long drink of the tepid but refreshing liquid, which tasted like stones.

Then he topped off his canteen, filled his cartridge loops from the box in his saddlebags, draped the bags and saddle over one shoulder, the scabbard and canteen over the other shoulder, heaved a weary sigh, pulled his hat brim low against the quickly dropping sun, and began walking in the direction he'd been heading before the ambush.

For happenstances such as this, he preferred low-heeled cavalry boots to the higher-heeled boots worn by most Westerners. It didn't take him long, tramping over the rough terrain, to mentally pat himself on the back for his choice. Regular stockmen's boots would have strangled his feet after a couple of hundred yards.

Still, an hour and maybe three-and-a-half, four miles later, his dogs were barking. They felt swollen one size larger. The heat of the desert had penetrated to his ankles. He paused to rest on a rock, took a few sips from his canteen, choked back the pain in his feet, and pushed on across the rocky desert, following the sun as though intending to meet it at its intersection with the earth though the western horizon was a lumpy violent patch of mountains—the Guadalupes. The range turned darker and darker as the afternoon wore on.

The heat, however, did not seem to abate in the least.

Longarm felt relieved when only a thumbnail-sized wedge of bloodred sun shone above the ever-darkening range. Then the dry breeze began to freshen against his face. He'd been watching for game for the past hour, and now he saw a jackrabbit foraging beneath an ocotillo partly shaded by a red escarpment, and shot it.

He quickly field dressed the jack then stuffed it into one of his saddlebag pouches, the head with its huge ears dangling over the side, and continued walking until he came upon a small log cabin dug into the side of a dome-shaped bluff stippled with Spanish bayonet. There was a small shed with an attached corral left of the cabin. No stock animals in the corral. The place looked abandoned.

He was in a canyon with low, limestone walls but with jogs of hills all around—a good, sheltered place to camp. He let his saddlebags and saddle slide off his shoulder to the ground fronting the cabin, and slid the Winchester from its scabbard.

He racked a round into the chamber, glanced around him once more, then said to the closed timbered door, "Halloo the camp."

The only reply came from several songbirds perched atop the dilapidated corral.

Longarm tripped the leather-and-steel latch, nudged the door with his rifle barrel. It sagged inward.

The place was indeed vacant, and by the dust and grime coating the square, roughhewn table scored with the initials of likely every saddle tramp who'd called the place home for anywhere from a night to a season of line riding, it hadn't housed anyone for weeks. It smelled of mouse and bird shit and the sour must of warm air pent up for a long time.

There was a sheet-iron stove and a wood box beside it stacked with kindling and split cordwood. It was the custom of the country to leave cabins stocked for anyone in need, and Longarm was grateful not only for the wood but also for the three air-tight tins of green beans and tomatoes on one of the three kitchen shelves.

A cot abutted the rear wall on the cabin's right side, bedecked with a green wool army blanket and a moisture-stained pillow of blue-striped ticking.

Longarm had seen a fire ring a few yards before the front door, and after stowing all his gear on the cabin's cot, he went back outside with an armload of wood and kindling. He built a fire in the stone ring, and then sat down on one of the two upended sitting logs beside the ring, and skinned the jackrabbit, tossing the skin into a pile to be discarded later. He set the rabbit on a rock in the fire, added a tin of tomatoes, to make a stew of sorts, then unwrapped his arm.

He had his saddlebags at his feet, and now, exposing the six-inch slash across his arm, he peeled his bloody sleeve away from it and cleaned it out with water from his canteen, and a cotton cloth. The wound was only about a quarter-inch deep, and if he cleaned and wrapped it well, he'd live to fight another day.

Add attempting to assassinate a federal lawman to your list of offenses. Not that they'd string you higher than you're already due . . .

He'd nearly emptied his canteen in cleaning the wound, so, looping the canteen's lanyard over his shoulder, he scouted around the cabin for a spring. He found one back in the rocks flanking the humble place—a nice, round pool of cool, black water fed by a near-steady trickle oozing out of the agave-stippled rocks above and behind it. The water ran off from the pool to seep into the ground, but he found that the pool itself was cool and refreshing.

It tasted a little tangy, and if the water had come from

a creek, he'd have suspected possibly a dead creature upstream. But every spring had its own flavor, and this wasn't half-bad, and the water was cold, so he plunged his face in for a long, loin-girding pull.

When he walked back to the fire, he was surprised to see that the flames had burned down to an umber glow, and the sun was gone. Darkness had descended, with only a single, fast-diminishing streak of green in the sky, stars guttering all around it. It was almost as though time had leaped ahead forty-five minutes.

"Christ," he muttered, dropping to his knees and tossing more wood on the fire.

He'd overcooked the jackrabbit stew, but it still tasted good and nourishing as he hunkered over the pot, sitting on his log, rifle leaning against his right thigh. The freshly rebuilt fire danced before him, the flames resembling several thin, red women doing some savage dance for his entertainment, lewd expressions on their slender, angular faces.

He snorted at the thought, then frowned, wondering at the sudden mushy turn his consciousness had taken.

The night pitched around him slightly, and he had to spread his feet to keep from tumbling off his log. His stomach was a little queasy in spite of the stew he'd just filled it with. Suddenly, the hair along his spine prickled. He dropped the pot and his fork with a clatter, and bolted to his feet. Again, the ground pitched, and he stumbled forward and then sideways, catching himself, reaching for the Winchester but missing it.

It dropped to the ground, the barrel pinging off the stewpot.

He snaked his right hand across his belly for his Colt, but he felt a tug and a sudden lightening of the weight on his left hip. When his hand brushed his holster, there was nothing there but leather. The hogleg was gone.

He smelled something . . . a person . . . behind him.

He turned, heavy on his feet.

Hazel eyes stared up at him catlike from beneath a broad hat brim. Breasts rose and fell slowly behind a cream and brown calico blouse. The gold chain to which a gold, turquoise-studded locket dangled was caressed by rich tufts of brunette hair. Longarm's own gun was rammed against his belly, and he reached for it with a grunt but stayed his hands when he saw that the hammer was cocked.

"Prepare to meet your maker, Deputy Long," said the husky voice of the demonic, chillingly beautiful young lady before him.

Chapter 11

Out the corner of his left eye, Longarm saw movement. He turned from the woman who had the gun rammed against his gut, to see three more just as vixenishly beautiful standing about ten feet beyond the fire. Four horses stood ground-reined behind them.

The women—two blondes and a Mexican—all stood facing him with their thumbs hooked behind their cartridge belts. One of the blondes—the blonder of the blondes—had a pair of doeskin gloves tucked behind her pearl gun handle. Firelight and dusky shadows flickered across his unexpected visitors, just beyond the warm air shimmering around the cook fire, so that Longarm, whose head swam as though he'd rolled down a steep hill, wondered if they were figments of his imagination.

The gun barrel poking his guts wasn't in his head, however. The hazel-eyed brunette twisted the gun around until Longarm had removed his hands from around the gun and took one wobbly step back.

"You poisoned the spring," he told the brunette.

The others sauntered toward him with maddening ease. The Mexican grinned, brown eyes flashing reflected firelight. "Oh, I wouldn't call it poison. We just flavored it up with something special."

"Very special," said the girl with wheat blond hair and clear blue eyes. She was likely the one who'd ambushed him earlier.

The strawberry blonde walked up and pressed her breasts against Longarm's left arm, ran a finger across the fresh bandage over the wound. "Something to make your arm feel better."

She grinned maliciously as she leaned farther forward and pressed her hand against his crotch, cupping his balls through his pants. "Something to make all of you feel better."

Longarm's crotch tingled. It took him aback. One of these ravishing killers had his gun rammed hard against his belly; another had her hand on his balls. And he was feeling warm blood surge into his loins, making his cock itch.

He'd never known both fear and desire at the same time, one emotion as powerful as the other.

"What was in it?" He slid his eyes around the women, and blinked to keep their images from separating and becoming two. "Had to be some powerful shit."

"Absynthe. And a wine made from cactus blossoms and peyote," said the brunette, holding the gun taut against his belly and lifting her chin up toward his own, enunciating each word perfectly, menacingly.

The Mexican stepped up beside the brunette, running the tip of her tongue along the underside of her upper lip as she held up her right hand, using her thumb and index finger to indicate a small amount. "And just a little bit of the venom milked from a female tarantula. Powerful . . . very powerful"—she ran her tongue across her lip again— "male stimulant."

"Aphrodisiac," said the blonde with her hand on his balls. "Been used by the Comanche for a thousand years. More effective than Spanish fly."

The brunette said, "That's why you never run into a sad Comanche squaw."

She and the other women laughed.

The brunette cut her laugh abruptly off, snarling and jabbing the gun hard against Longarm's belly, just up from his crotch. "Take your clothes off. Every stitch. Starting with the gunbelt. And don't try anything. We gave you just enough absinthe and peyote to keep you physically unable to run away . . ."

"And just enough of the tarantula venom," the Mexican added, "to keep you from wanting to."

"Holy shit," said the strawberry blonde, widening her eyes as she stared at Longarm's crotch. "He's already growing a hard one. A *big*, hard one."

Longarm ignored the numb pull in his groin. "What the hell you women want?"

"You know what we want," said the strawberry blonde, who lowered his hand from his crotch and backed away as though to get a better look at him. "Ain't that obvious enough for you? You ain't a virgin, are you, big boy?"

She and the others chuckled. Longarm's ears warmed with embarrassment and anger. He'd be damned if these four weren't getting to him. He almost felt as though they were stabbing little stilettos in him, all over his body. He couldn't move. He was powerless. And the pain he was feeling was all the more frustrating and maddening for being pleasing, as well.

The brunette rammed his gun into his belly harder, gritting her teeth. "Take your clothes off. Or I'll gut-shoot you, lawman!"

Longarm grunted and stepped back again though he was getting closer and closer to the fire. He looked at the other women. They all had their pistols out now, too. Their hammers cocked, lips quirking malevolent smiles. Silver trimmings on their colorful vaquero garb flashed in the firelight, nearly blinding him.

Longarm fumbled with his cartridge belt, let it drop at his feet. Staring at the guns rather than at the pretty, wicked faces before him, he kicked out of a boot, nearly stumbling back into the fire as he did. He kicked off the other one more carefully then unbuttoned his pants, becoming aware to his poignant humiliation that he was fully hard, his mast pushing painfully against his underwear.

His pulse throbbed in his ears. Fury raged in him beneath the surging heat in his loins.

He removed his shirt and then his summer-weight balbriggans. Finally, he gave his hat a toss onto his clothes piled up beside the fire.

All four women were staring at his piston-hard cock slanting up in front of him, bobbing slightly with each beat of his heart. The head was an oversized purple mushroom.

"*Cristo*," whispered the señorita, ramming her gun into its holster then moving quickly to unbuckle her cartridge belt.

The others stepped back away from Longarm and began undressing in a lusty frenzy, their wide eyes raking the tall, brawny, well-muscled, battle-scarred lawman before them.

Now was his chance. They'd soon be as naked as he was. Already their pistols were on the ground. A glance toward their horses waiting ground-reined at the edge of the flickering firelight told him their rifles were still snugged down in their saddle scabbards.

As the women hastily shucked off their clothes, Longarm took a step forward then half feigned dropping to his knees. He needed to get low enough to make a quick grab for one of their weapons. With his head spinning, he couldn't leap for one, or he'd fall flat on his face. He did not have to feign light-headedness. The girls undressing before him were splitting in twos and threes and pitching this way and that. His head bobbled drunkenly; he blinked, trying to clear his vision. He glanced at the brunette's pearl-gripped Colt snugged inside a soft, brown leather holster trimmed with a glistening silver star.

That was the one he'd go for.

He slid his gaze to the left of the gun, saw a narrow ankle tapering up to a well-turned calf glowing gold in the firelight. The brunette's foot was long and slender, the toes perfectly formed. The tops of her feet were pale; underneath, they were the pink of a smooth baby's ass.

His cock throbbed, burned with desire.

He had to ignore it. He had to keep his attention fixed on the gun.

Letting his eyes slide up the brunette's legs, he began crawling toward her, intending to spring sharply at the last second for the ivory-handled Colt in her holster. His eyes crawled on up her thighs to the dark V between her legs, wisps of brunette hair curling out slightly from the welcoming tuft. Suddenly, he heard the brunette give her husky laugh as he wrapped his arms around her legs and buried his face in her snatch.

She gave a catlike mewl and dug her hands in his hair, pressing his face harder against her snatch.

"Oh," she said as he poked his tongue between her legs, parting the tender, petal-like folds of flesh. "Oh, *ohhh . . .*"

He glanced at the pistol. As much as he wanted to make a grab for it, he couldn't draw himself away from the woman, who suddenly knelt before him while another ran her hands through his hair from behind while the other two knelt to either side of him, rubbing their full, firm breasts against his shoulders.

While the brunette kissed him hungrily, the strawberry blonde reached between his legs, sliding one of her hands up and down his cock while massaging her pussy with the other.

"Oh, God," she said. "Look how he's hung. He's a fucking Brahma bull. Girls, feel his balls . . ."

They all felt his balls, tugging and pulling his cock and making it even harder, making it throb with more vigor, if that was possible. His head spun, but the lips, hands, breasts, and furry snatches of the girls were an elixir every bit as intoxicating as the concoction they'd spiked his water hole with. The firelight and flickering shadows added to the otherworldly quality of the orgy.

And orgy it was. When the brunette pulled her lips away from his, she fell backward, drawing him toward her while two of the other girls, one on each side, guided his raging hard-on between the brunette's madly expanding and sopping snatch.

The Mexican chuckled as Longarm began to ride the brunette. She collapsed on top of him, squirming around on his back while he fucked the brunette, who groaned and grunted and thrashed, flapping her bent knees like the wings of some large bird trying desperately to become airborne.

Swathed in sexual bliss that grew more and more intense with each thrust of his powerful hips, sliding his cock in and out of the howling brunette, Longarm tried to delay his climax as long as he could. If it hadn't been for the spiked water hole, he'd have had an easier time of it. He'd only ridden the brunette five or six minutes (or so he thought, his sense of time being as befuddled as all his other senses) before he arched his head and back and loosed a lion-like wail as he let go, his ass and hips spasming and his seed jetting into the girl's hot, wet canal.

She ground her heels into his back and pulled his hair. On top of him, the Mexican screamed and chewed one of his earlobes. She smeared him with her own wet crotch. The other girls cooed and groaned, massaging their own breasts, squeezing their nipples, squealing.

"I'm next," said the Mexican, rolling off Longarm's back until she lay beside the snapping fire, taking her knees in her hands and spreading her long, cherry red legs as wide as she could without dislocating her hips.

Longarm looked down between his own legs. His cock appeared every bit as stiff as before. Glistening wet, and piston-hard. He shook his head. That was some aphrodisiac they'd given him. If he'd been a little clearer in his head, he might have been angry. As it was, his fury had dissipated. He was thoroughly consumed by the liquid drug as well as the drug of these dancing, writhing, firelit beauties clinging to his brawny, sweaty frame like worker bees to a honeycomb.

He fucked the Mexican until she lay quivering and screeching epithets in Spanish. He took the strawberry blonde next. He left her sobbing. The wheat blonde insisted on blowing him; she was expert at it.

While she worked her magical lips and tongue up and down his throbbing shaft, hefting his balls, the others took turns kissing him, mingling their tongues with his. He had no idea how much later he found himself on his knees, holding the brunette's hips in his hands while he took her from behind. The others swarmed around on them, playing with the brunette's and each other's breasts or pressing their own tits against Longarm's thrusting ass.

And then the sex-drunk lawman found himself on his back, three beauties slumped, exhausted, across his chest, arms, and legs, while the wheat blonde, naked and sweaty as a stone-age savage, her hair mussed and covered with dirt, grit, and burrs, dropped a fresh armload of wood onto the fire.

She looked down at him through the leaping flames. Her teeth were impossibly white in her perfect, high-cheekboned face. Her eyes glowed. She smiled.

Longarm groaned. Sleep pressed down on him. He tried to hold it at bay. If he slept, he'd surely die. These sexy savages would shoot him or stick a knife in him.

Nevertheless, his eyelids dropped, heavy as andirons. He sighed, and slept . . .

Chapter 12

Someone was holding a railroad spike to the top of Long-arm's head. Someone else was using a sledgehammer to smash the spike through his skull and into his brain plate, and farther. Into his jaws . . . into his neck and shoulders . . .

He opened his eyes then closed them again at the painful rush of garish morning light. He hooked his arms over his head and pressed down, trying to shield himself from the spike and that consarned hammer that just wouldn't quit.

Suddenly, hardening his jaws against the pain, he forced his eyes open and lifted his head. His camp was awash with the light of morning. Midmorning. There were few shadows. To his right, his cook fire was a mound of white ash, a few thin tendrils of smoke curling above two chunks of fire-blackened wood. Around the ring, the ground was scuffed and scored. It bore the in-dentations of knees and buttocks.

That was all that remained of the women who'd visited him last night. They themselves were gone. Only a few piles of fresh apples remained where their horses had been ground-tied at the edge of the firelight.

Longarm raised a hand to his chest as to make sure a knife had not been shoved through his heart, as he'd been so certain would happen if he slept. He ran both hands through his rumpled hair, vaguely wondering if the pain in his skull was caused by a bullet. No. There was no hole, no blood. Only the miserable pain of that spike and sledgehammer wielded by a grinning giant.

Longarm looked down at himself. He was naked. There was a blanket on either side of him, but he'd been so sound asleep that he hadn't used either one to ward off the desert chill that still lingered in the air though the rising sun was heating up quickly. He leaned back on his elbows, wincing against the thudding in his head, and smacked his lips, taking stock of his situation and all that had happened last night.

Had he really been visited by the Four Horsewomen of the Apocalypse, or had he merely been dreaming? Wet-dreaming like the randiest of twelve-year-old boys?

He grabbed his cock. It alone would have told the story if his aching head hadn't. If his mouth, dry as parched rawhide and tasting like a slop bucket, hadn't. His drooping dong was chafed and raw and still tacky with the myriad sexual fluids of those four bewitching demons who'd poisoned his spring, made him as hard as a rogue grizzly just clambering out of his winter den on the first day of a Rocky Mountain spring.

By God, they'd ravaged the holy hell out of him!

Though he'd enjoyed it nearly as much as they obviously had. And judging by their screams, howls, and whimpers, they obviously had. And since he'd given up trying to defend himself so early and just thrown himself to the wolves, so to speak . . .

But his enjoyment had been induced by the intoxicating concoction they'd poisoned his spring with. They'd kept him as hard as oak for most of the night, clamoring around him for more, more, more. Even waking him from stupors to crawl atop him and impale themselves on his still raging hard-on. When they'd had their fill, they'd left sometime after he'd last fallen asleep.

Why hadn't they killed him? They must have known he was here to hunt them. After all, they'd sent Grogan Caulfield to bore a gourd-sized hole through his brisket.

Longarm pressed the heels of his hands to his temples and shook his head. Befuddling. Damn befuddling.

There was no point in puzzling over it at the moment, however. His thinker box was cloudy and ringing with each blast of that grinning sadist's hammer. Water. He needed water, but he obviously couldn't drink from the spring. He spied his canteen, which he remembered he hadn't filled from the spring, thank God, and rinsed his mouth out with several mouthfuls before taking a long pull of the stale but refreshing liquid.

The water helped to ease the thunder in his head. Thinking a little more fluidly now, he looked around for his clothes. They weren't where he'd remembered leaving them.

Stumbling around barefoot, grunting against the sharp rocks and thorns, he spied a boot lying at the western edge of the camp. He went over and picked it up, and saw his other boot lying another twenty yards beyond. That one had both socks in it. Stealing forward tenderly on feet that still bore the blisters of yesterday's long tramp, and even more sensitive than usual to the goat-heads and other sharp thorns carpeting the West Texas desert, he continued hot-footing out from his camp, picking up one article of clothing at a time.

Balbriggans, neckerchief, pants, shirt, vest, and finally, his hat. They were having fun with him, taunting him, humiliating him. The forced hard-on and tumble hadn't been enough. Looking around, holding his clothes and boots against his belly, he wondered if they were around somewhere, watching him, laughing and clapping each other on the back for a job well done.

If they were, they were doing a good job of keeping out of sight. Nothing around but the rolling, sotol-bristling desert and the sand-colored ridges beyond.

And his gunbelt. He saw the flash of the buckle, and when he'd dressed and eased his battered, blistered feet into his boots, he walked over and, sure enough, they'd left his shell belt and holstered Colt coiled on a flat rock about twenty yards from where he'd found his hat. Another glance around revealed his rifle leaning against a lone desert willow in which a hawk perched, watching this human fool with dull curiosity.

He checked the loads in his Winchester. Fully loaded. Why? Another taunt? Were they saying, "Sure, we know you're out here, lawman. Thanks for the fuck. Oh, and here's your pistol and loaded Winchester. Good hunting!"

Longarm shouldered the rifle and walked back toward the cabin. He rolled his blankets, tied them to his saddle, then shouldered his gear and set out once more for Santa Clara. His ears burned. Not because of the rising, stoking sun. But because he could hear them laughing at him from wherever they may have been.

The final nail in the coffin of his self-esteem came when, after he'd walked a mile, he came to a wash and found a cream horse with black spots splashed across its hindquarters tied to a gnarled cottonwood. The gelding eyed him warily, snorted, and stomped one rear hoof.

Longarm dropped his saddle and saddlebags, and raised his rifle, looking around. But it was unlikely the four women would be setting a trap for him now. If they'd wanted to kill him, they'd had plenty of opportunities. No, the horse was just another way of their telling him that they had no fear of him.

Maybe they even thought they'd get another chance to use him like they'd used him last night.

"Fat chance of that," he said, lowering the rifle.

He crouched to lift his saddle, but froze, frowning down at the McClellan and his saddlebags though what he was seeing in his mind's eye were the four women— their hair, their teeth, their heaving bosoms, their nicely rounded hips tapering to long, slender legs. But what made the picture peculiar were their faces. Or the lack of their faces. The women were like a photograph in his mind, with the faces blotted out or blurred beyond recognition.

Longarm straightened, his brows mantling his narrowed eyes in consternation. He stared off unseeing, trying to focus on the women once more. He wanted to remember what they looked like so that when he saw them again, he'd recognize them. Try as he might, the faces remained blurry.

He chuffed wryly, ran a hand down his face as though to clear his vision. "What the hell? I can see everything about those four, includin' the color of their hair. But for the life of me, I can't remember their faces."

He remembered what Whip Freeman had said about the four women maybe being demons. Could it be?

He chuffed again. He was just exhausted and hung-over. What he needed was a good soak in a hot tub, some liniment rubbed into his feet, and a long nap followed by a good meal with all the trimmings. The rest and food would run off that sadist with the sledge-hammer in his head, and he'd likely remember the women's faces. And he'd be on the hunt once more.

Only this time he'd be the one springing the trap, by God . . .

Wearily, he saddled the cream, tying down his rifle scabbard. Just as wearily, he climbed into the saddle and started off at a spanking trot, gritting his teeth against the hammer-wielding sadist. He was a little surprised to see that the horse seemed to know the direction Long-arm was heading. Or maybe it could smell the town, and wanted to head that way, as well.

The gelding didn't require much direction throughout the rest of the long morning. At a fork in the trail that the horse had discovered itself, the cream did not hesitate before angling off on the right tine, heading southwest around the shoulder of a rocky hill.

A half hour later, Longarm saw the roofs of Santa Clara rise from the rolling desert, flanked by the bulging, blue-green peaks of the Guadalupes. So the horse did know where it was going. The reason became clear when, entering town from the east, a voice called from Long-arm's right, "Good Lord! Where'd you find him?"

Longarm reined the horse to a halt and turned to see the banker, Angus Whitehurst, standing outside the small, stone, tile-roofed Santa Clara Bank & Trust, which sat alone on its own lot, fronted by a humble brush-roofed gallery. The banker wore a light green suit with a match-ing planter's hat, and he had a long, black cigar in his beringed right hand, the dark cigar making the banker's hand look all the more pale in contrast.

A prim but attractive young woman with strawberry blonde hair wearing a conservative black frock flanked him, holding a covered wicker basket on the shaded gallery. Wearing a small, felt hat adorned with fake cherries, she followed Whitehurst with her curious eyes as he strode off the gallery and into the street toward Longarm.

"Go on in, Mrs. Kelly," the banker said, glancing at her over his shoulder. "Make yourself at home in my private office, and I'll be there to discuss your husband's accounts in a moment."

Longarm looked at the woman. Her eyes met his and held there for one long second before she turned quickly away, her neck above the starched collar of her shirtwaist coloring slightly. Longarm kept his eyes on the woman's slender back and narrow but firm shoulders as she turned away from him and walked into the bank.

A worm of suspicion flicked its tail in Longarm's gut. Could she have been one of . . . Nah. Couldn't be. He'd just been fucked one too many times last night, drunk too much of that tarantula juice the demons had poisoned the spring with, and now he'd likely look for those demons in every woman he saw. There had to be more than one strawberry blond in Guadalupe County.

He glanced down at Whitehurst, who stood just off his left stirrup, staring up at him. He'd been saying something, but Longarm's thoughts had been on the strawberry blonde, though now he could hear the banker repeating, "Where did you find him? Where? That's my horse . . . the one that was pulling my surrey that day those four women robbed me!"

Longarm looked down at the cream as though seeing him for the first time. "No kiddin'?"

"Of course I'm not kidding! Where on earth did you find him, Deputy Long?"

Longarm wasn't about to tell the man—or any man— what had happened last night. Never. He wouldn't even mutter his shame on his deathbed. But that didn't mean he had to lie about the banker's horse. "He was tied to a tree out in the middle of nowhere. Just happened along on him, and there he was."

"Where's *your* horse?"

"That there is a long, damn story." Longarm swung down from his saddle, and quickly unbuckled his McClellan's belly strap. He slipped the saddle and saddlebags from the cream, shouldering the gear, and swung around toward the hotel sitting farther up the street and on the opposite side. "There's your horse, Whitehurst."

Behind him, the banker said, "But where . . . What . . ."

"Don't look a gift horse in the mouth, Whitehurst," Longarm said without turning around.

Chapter 13

The gear on his shoulders weighing a ton, Longarm pushed through the doors of the Guadalupe House hotel and tramped across the deep plush carpet toward the gleaming oak desk at the rear of the lobby and near the stairs rising to the second and third stories.

Hearing a hard brushing sound on his right, he glanced through the broad open doorway into the dining room. Mrs. Pringle was setting silverware on one of the round, white-clothed tables near the door while a girl in a dark blue uniform dress and white apron was down on her hands and knees, scrubbing at the thick blood-stain on the carpet, where Longarm had dropped his shotgun-wielding, would-be assassin, Grogan Caulfield.

He tapped his fingers on the barrel of the Winchester resting on his right shoulder. In all of last night's com-motion, he'd forgot about Caulfield and his so-called message from the Four Horsewomen of the Apocalypse. Why had they sent the old gun-handy Indian agent after Longarm? The women were certainly capable of doing the dirty deed themselves. Of course, they'd had ample opportunity last night, but they hadn't followed through. Or had they intended to kill him but decided to let him live and only humiliate him instead, knowing they'd soon get another chance at him?

Confident bitches, he'd give them that.

Still, why had they involved Caulfield?

Longarm looked at Matilda Pringle. She'd stopped setting the silver on the table to gaze at him curiously, shallow lines carved across her pretty forehead. Longarm felt a hitch in his chest, similar to the sudden nudge of apprehension he'd felt in the street a few minutes ago, when he'd seen the strawberry blonde known as Mrs. Kelly.

The hazel eyes held the lawman's skeptical, brown-eyed gaze. Had he seen those eyes last night, staring up at him while he'd toiled between the woman's long legs, her supple form writhing beneath him as she'd moaned like a lust-drunk wildcat? Indeed, could Mrs. Pringle be last night's brunette? She appeared very prim and starched today, of course, in her elegant purple velvet gown, pearl necklace, and with her thick hair drawn tightly back behind her head and secured in a fist-sized bun.

But she certainly had the height and the ripe-breasted swell of the hazel-eyed brunette.

By the same token, could Mrs. Kelly be one of last night's two blondes? The woman Longarm had seen on the bank's stoop had been roughly their same height, if Longarm remembered correctly through the lingering fog of the evil concoction he'd lapped so unwittingly from the spring. But there were plenty of blondes of differing shades around Santa Clara. He'd already seen them. Plenty of brunettes, too. Damn, if only he had a clear picture of their faces . . .

"Are you all right, Deputy Long. I mean . . ." She flushed slightly. "Longarm . . ."

He was staring at her. Her ruby lips were parted in a skeptical smile. If she had been one of the women he'd fucked last night, she was a damn good actress. Had nonchalance down to a science.

Longarm shifted his gaze to the girl still scrubbing near the table he and the town councilmen had been sitting at. She grunted quietly with the effort of trying to get Grogan Caulfield's blood up out of the carpet.

"He leaked a little, ole Grogan."

"He certainly did." Mrs. Pringle gave a little shudder as she turned toward the girl doing the scrubbing. "I think the rug is ruined, quite frankly."

Longarm couldn't help studying her further. Those hazel eyes. Her voice didn't sound as raspy as the one he'd heard last night, mewling beneath him. Or did it?

"How's your husband?"

"Oh, he'll be all right. The doctor plucked the buckshot out of his arm and bandaged him up. Only minor wounds." She sighed. "He's taken to bed, however. Poor man was somewhat traumatized, I'm afraid."

She paused then wrinkled the skin at the bridge of her nose. "You didn't fetch your room key last night."

"No. I ended up spendin' the night out in the desert."

What appeared genuine surprise shone on the pretty woman's face. "Oh? You look sunburned. Could you use a bath?"

"I could at that. Reckon I'd be obliged if you sent a tub and water to my room. Figure I'll nap later, come down for some vittles around supper time."

"Lizzy is busy here," said Matilida Pringle. "I'll fetch your water myself."

"Thank you." Longarm pinched his hat brim, thinking it odd the hotel owner's wife would haul water, and started up the lobby. He stopped and turned to Mrs. Pringle still watching him obliquely through the open door. "You know anything about Mrs. Kelly?" He stared at her, maintaining a stone face, waiting to see how she'd take the bait.

The hotel owner's wife hiked a shoulder. "Only that she's a very nice, respectable young lady. A churchgoing woman. Raises a few chickens behind her and her husband Jack's place. Or I should say what used to be her and Jack's place. The poor man died yesterday afternoon."

"Oh?"

"Yes. Heart seizure, I'm afraid. He hadn't been well."

"I see." Longarm kept his voice noncommittal.

"See what, Longarm?"

He stared at her, letting her know in his own oblique that he was suspicious. Might be dangerous, but no more dangerous than what he'd been through last night. How could he find out if she really was the sensuous, lust-crazed brunette in the pack of four he'd tussled with?

Feeling sheepish and embarrassed, he finally turned away from the woman. She wasn't giving anything away by her words or her expression. He strode on over to the desk and she hurried up behind him, passing him. He got a good look at her fanny pulling the purple velvet dress taut in a most pleasing way.

The brunette he'd gotten Biblical with had had a nice ass. Taut but full, just enough flesh for a man to grab and hold on to. Longarm found himself undressing Mrs.

Pringle with his eyes, wondering what she'd look like sans the purple velvet, pearls, and likely a corset, pantaloons, and camisole. And let her hair down . . .

"Are you sure you're all right, Deputy?" she said, frowning at him as she held his brass room key over the polished oak desk at the foot of the carpeted stairs. "You're acting . . . strangely. Too much sun?"

"Yep."

Longarm closed his hand around the key that she dropped into his palm then, hefting his gear once more, tramped on up the stairs. In his room, he dropped his gear on the canopied bed, pegged his hat, shrugged out of his sweaty, grimy shirt, and dropped it on the floor.

He fished his bottle out of his saddlebags, plucked the cork out with his teeth, and tramping toward one of the room's two windows, took a long pull. God, but rye tasted good when the weight of the world settled hard and fast! Those two deep, burning swallows instantly swathed him in mind-dumbing comfort, burning out the last vestiges of last night's hangover, obliterating the sadistic giant's hammer, and slowing everything down.

His thoughts moving more slowly now, he slid a gauzy red curtain aside and stared down into the main street of Santa Clara.

A couple of farm wagons were lumbering along, just now passing each other as they headed in opposite directions, dust rising in the hot air. Looking eastward, Longarm's attention held on the strawberry blonde just now stepping off the bank's front gallery and moving toward him on the street's opposite side. She had the dour expression of the married, town-dwelling woman—a woman whose days were likely spent scrubbing floors and hoeing a garden in the Texas heat, cooking meals, doing laundry, tending children, and pleasing her husband.

A woman who squeezed little pleasure from her hard existence.

Or that was the expression she wore. Stony. Eyes for the most part downcast. Nah, she hadn't been the strawberry blonde from last night—ripe and horny and throwing herself at Longarm's dong with wild abandon. For him to suspect her meant he really had gotten too much sun.

He was about to lift the bottle again, when, as the woman passed the hotel and stepped down off a boardwalk fronting a drugstore, she glanced sharply to her right, eyes raking the upper stories of the hotel. For half a second, her eyes met Longarm's, and held.

Of course, she couldn't see the lawman in the window. Or could she? As if she had seen him, she turned her head forward quickly and continued on across the mouth of a cross street, a small beaded purse swinging down around her pleated cream skirt bustling about her legs. He couldn't see much of her, concealed as she was by the conservatively cut housedress, but she was obviously a well-set-up woman. Prim expressions could disguise a nice bust and rump.

Longarm lifted the bottle to his lips, took a slow, thoughtful pull. Hearing footsteps in the hall, he set the bottle down and was just turning toward the door when the knock came.

"Deputy Long?" came Matilda's Pringle's sexily raspy voice. "Are you decent and presentable?"

I am, Longarm thought with an amused chuff. How 'bout you, Mrs. Pringle?

"Come in."

The woman opened the door. Beside her stood a raw-boned boy with a rumpled mop of red-brown hair in broadcloth trousers, suspenders, and a hickory shirt. The lad was holding a high-backed copper washtub. The boy came in and set the tub on the floor.

"Bring up two buckets of water," Mrs. Pringle told the boy. "Then go on back to the kitchen, Albert. I'll haul the rest for Deputy Long."

The boy went out.

"The cook needs wood for the kitchen range," the woman told Longarm as she began turning again toward the hall, pulling the door closed. "So I'll be bringing your water up, Deputy."

"So I heard."

"If you'll be so kind as to remain . . . presentable."

"You mean you want me to keep my clothes on till you're done?"

She glanced back at him, arching a brow in perplexed surprise. "Yes, of course that's what I mean." She went out, drawing the door closed behind her. Longarm stood in front of the window, holding the bottle, feeling foolish, distrustful. But he had every reason to feel distrustful. The four women had to be somewhere, and what better place for them to hide than right here in town, in plain sight?

He had to find out if Matilda Pringle was one of them.

He sat on the bed, drinking whiskey, until the kid had brought up two buckets of water—one hot, one cold. When the kid had hightailed it back to the kitchen, Longarm climbed off the bed and began shucking out of his clothes. He tossed everything into a pile by the door then hunkered down in the tub. He wore only his hat. Reaching for a half-smoked cheroot, he lit it then sat back in the tub, hands on the sides, waiting.

What if Mrs. Pringle was the husky-voiced demon? She might try to kill him. He wouldn't put anything past any of those lovely she-demons. Did she have a weapon concealed in her dress? There were certainly enough frilly pleats and folds in which to hide one . . .

Longarm stood and reached for his Colt snugged down in the holster hooked around a near bedpost. Because of a lumber drey clattering loudly on the street below his window, he didn't hear the woman's tread in the hall, and he didn't hear the knock on the door until she'd already pushed it open. He turned to her, naked and dripping.

She'd had her head down, wrestling with the water bucket in her hands, but now she lifted her head, and stopped. Her hazel eyes widened with a start. Her lips parted.

"Longarm!"

He set his Colt on the floor on the tub's right side, and sank down into the lukewarm water. "Sorry, there, Mrs. Pringle. Just wanted to grab my hogleg. Never know who might be on the prowl in Santa Clara." He rolled the cigar from one corner of his mouth to the other. "If'n you know what I mean?"

She set the bucket on the floor and turned her head to one side, shielding her eyes with her hand. "You knew I was returning with more water. Why on earth did you disrobe?"

"I reckon I forgot you was comin'."

"This is most inappropriate. You know it is!"

Longarm puffed smoke around the cheroot in his mouth, and closed his hands over his cock and balls.

"Go ahead and dump it in here. I've covered all my nasty parts."

"If someone should see . . ."

"Might wanna close the door." He grinned, continuing to send smoke plumes billowing around his hatted head.

Giving him her back, she closed the door. Dropping her eyes to the floor, she picked up the bucket, hustled it on over to Longarm, and averting her troubled gaze, her cheeks mottled red, poured the water into the tub.

"There you are," she said stiffly, swinging around.

"Just one thing, ma'am." Longarm sank back in the tub again, removing his hands from his crotch. He plucked the cheroot from his mouth, and studied the gray coal. "Where were you last evening, if you don't me askin'?"

She turned from the door, frowning indignantly. "Why on earth—"

"Oh, it ain't idle curiosity, Mrs. Pringle. It's more on the professional side."

"Well, I . . . I . . ." She looked confused, flustered, hazel eyes flashing with reflected window light.

"Yes?"

"I went to the church for several hours, right after supper. Then I came home, squared up my accounting books, tidied the dining room, and went to bed."

"Was your husband here?"

"He was over at the Mountain View Saloon, as he is most nights after six thirty or so. My husband has a weakness for gambling, Deputy Long. Now, if you'll excuse me . . ."

"Not just yet."

"You cannot keep me here. Why—you're naked!"

"Don't you want to know why I'm asking about your whereabouts, Mrs. Pringle?"

"Oh, I'm sure you have your reasons. You're a law-man. And you've been out in the sun too long." She stared at him, her hand on the doorknob. "Are you going to tell me?"

"You don't know?"

"Did someone rob the bank?"

"You have any idea who those four kill-crazy women around here are? Where they come from?"

"Certainly *not*!"

Longarm stared at her, rolling the cigar around in his mouth, openly raking his eyes across her. Her breasts didn't look quite as full as the girl's from last night, but she was of a similar build, with the same color hair and eyes. The mouth wasn't quite right, but different clothes and a different hairstyle could make the entire person appear different. But after last night's strenuous tumble, wouldn't she look tired? He had to admit she appeared relatively well rested.

Longarm's scrutiny brought a richer flush to her cheeks. Her own eyes flicked across his shoulders and upper arms, and then with a quiet gasp, as though catching herself, she dropped her gaze to the floor and swung toward the door, which she opened. "If you'll forgive me, I have work to do, Deputy Long."

"Longarm."

"Whatever!" She rushed out and closed the door. The door opened again. She came in and looked down at his clothes piled on the floor. "Do you want me to have these laundered for you?"

"I'd be obliged."

She gathered up the soiled duds without looking at

him, stuffed them into her empty water bucket, and went out.

Longarm gave the cigar a final roll between his lips.

If she'd been one of those who'd frolicked with him last night in the desert, she was a damn good actress.

Late that night, Longarm lifted his head from his pillow. He'd heard something. The tap came again. Automatically, Longarm flung a hand toward the poster on which he'd hung his gun and cartridge belt, and clicked back the hammer of his .44.

He growled, "You best be friendly, or you're gonna be dead before you hear this hogleg pop."

Chapter 14

"Mister . . . I mean, Longarm?" came Matilda's voice through the hotel room door, raised just above a whisper. "I . . . I have your clothes."

"What clothes?"

Her voice trilled slightly. "The ones I had laundered for you."

Longarm chuckled quietly. He threw the bedcovers back, rose, and clad in only his threadbare spare long-handles that clung to his large, rangy frame like a second skin, walked to the door. He kept to one side, holding the Colt down low, and aimed at the knob as he drew the door open a foot.

She was silhouetted against the lights from a couple of coal oil bracket lamps. Her face was a pale smudge framed by her hair hanging loose about her shoulders. There was an inverted V of more skin exposed by the wrap she wore. She held his clothes, all folded and smelling of soap and starch, before her.

"I know it's late." She hesitated. "I thought you might want them for tomorrow."

Longarm drew the door halfway open and beckoned her in with the Colt. "Best come in, lest folks see you out there . . . and get the wrong idea."

She sucked at her upper lip then stepped into the room. Longarm closed the door, set the gun on a dresser, and took the clothes from her. He stood before her, towering over her, looking down at her, smelling her freshly washed and brushed hair. Setting his clothes on a chair, he went over to the dresser, removed the chimney on the red hurricane lamp, and lit it.

He turned up the wick until she came into view before him, clad in a flowered red and yellow wrap. She wore some dainty silk slippers, a bow across the toes. He saw a good foot of ankle and calf. He wanted to see more.

"Well, you're still here," he said.

She kept her eyes on the floor. Her hair hid her face. Her bosom rose and fell slowly, heavily, as she breathed. She was much fuller than she'd appeared in the dress she wore earlier. Likely, a corset had trussed her breasts up tight against her chest. Now, he doubted she wore a thing beneath the wrap.

"Where's your husband?"

"Gambling." Her voice was a whisper but he could still hear the faintly husky rasp in it. "He won't be back till morning."

"Where's the prim married woman who filled my tub earlier?"

She looked up at him now. Her hazel eyes shone in the flickering red light from the lamp. They appeared cat-like, predatory. He found himself wondering if she'd concealed a derringer under the wrap.

"What—you want to humiliate me? My husband can't satisfy me. He never has. It's not his fault. He drinks and smokes and stays out too late. And he's older than me by twenty years. Is it so wrong to want to feel like a woman?"

"How do you know I can make you feel that way?" He was still trying to puzzle her out. Was she here to fuck him or kill him?

Or both?

Only one way to find out.

He stepped forward, pulled the cloth belt knotted around her waist. The wrap fell apart, hung from her shoulders, exposing a long vertical line, eight inches wide, from her throat to the darkly furred tuft between her legs and the insides of her thighs. She drew a sharp, audible breath but made no effort to pull the wrap closed.

"Christ, you're more beautiful than you let on during the day, Mrs. Pringle."

"I didn't figure you being a talker, Longarm."

Longarm slid the robe down off her shoulders. It fell to the floor. She moved toward him, stepping out of her slippers.

He placed his hands over her breasts, mentally comparing them to those of the hazel-eyed brunette from the night before, and closed his mouth over hers.

She kept her lips open, her chest falling faster and more heavily now as he rolled her nipples between his thumbs and index fingers. He kissed her for a time, sucking at her tongue, causing her to groan, and then nuzzled her neck, furtively searching for any marks he might have left there.

If he had, he saw no evidence of it. Later, he'd inspect her legs. As savagely as he and the Four Horsewomen of the Apocalypse had tussled on the bare ground, there must be some evidence if only for a scraped knee or a red ass. His own knees and ass were scraped, and his cock was still a little raw. He could feel it coming alive again now, though.

The damn thing had a mind of its own and it was rarely connected to the one in his head. All it knew was that he had a ripe, desirable, desirous woman in his arms, and it wanted to penetrate her . . .

When he'd nuzzled and inspected the woman's breasts, unable to come to any conclusions about her identity, he picked her up naked in his arms and lay her down on the bed. She lay still in the flickering shadows and red light, breathing through half-parted lips as he skinned out of his longhandles.

He watched her.

She stared back at him, breathing, waiting. There was none of the savagery he'd seen in the eyes of last night's brunette. He could tell she wanted him . . . or any man who could satisfy her at last . . . but there was also a hesitation in her gaze. Possibly an uncertainty, a fear that she herself might not perform to his standards.

He'd seen none of that in the eyes or demeanors of the four killers.

Growing more and more doubtful that this was the same savage brunette as last night, he walked over to her, dong jutting. She glanced down at it, swallowed, then spread her legs slightly as he climbed on top of her. He lowered his lips to her right breast, and chewed it gently while he spread her legs with his own, then used his hand to slide his cock through the warm, damp hair of her cunt, and penetrate her.

"Oh!" she gasped as he drove himself as deep as he could go.

She turned her head from left to right, making a pained expression. As he began bucking against her, she gasped once more then lifted her head and pressed her warm lips against his neck, biting him tenderly as he fucked her. She continued to keep her mouth close to his neck, sending her warm breath puffing against him, caressing his arms and shoulders with her fingertips.

It wasn't hard to bring her to climax. Maybe she really had been waiting for it for a long time. She shuddered and groaned, stuck two knuckles in her mouth, and bit down on them hard until he'd finally stopped pumping, and pulled out of her.

No, she couldn't be the same brunette he'd had last night. She'd been too easy to please, and been far too demure, civilized . . .

Unless, as Whip Freeman had suggested, she really was a demon . . .

He was exhausted, but she squirmed around beneath him and got him hard again. Now, that was more like the gal from last night . . .

What the hell? Her body was enticing, breasts full and wanting, the nipples distended. She urged him with her eyes. He decided to oblige her.

This time, he lifted her legs, placing both her calves on his left shoulder, going at her at a slightly different angle. She started out sighing then began groaning and hammering the bed with her fists as he brought her to climax once more.

"Do you mind if I stay here awhile?" she asked when they'd lain together in silence for a time.

"What about Mr. Pringle?"

"Like I said, he won't be back for a time. And there are no other guests in the hotel tonight." She frowned up at him, perplexed. "Why are you looking at me like that?"

"Like how?"

She laughed suddenly. "Like you think I'm going to stick a knife in your back!"

She threw her arms and legs around him, squeezing him hard and laughing almost demonically against his neck. "You really did have too much sun today, didn't you?"

"I reckon." Longarm had shuttled his gaze to her legs. "Matilda," he said thoughtfully, feeling a fresh twinge of apprehension. "Your knees are scraped." He ran his finger across the long, narrow scab running horizontally across her right knee. "How'd that happen?"

"Stop—you're making me self-conscious!" she chastised, turning onto her belly. "Some of us scrub kitchen floors for a living, Longarm." She wagged her ass and laughed huskily, shaking her hair out across her pillow and causing an icicle of apprehension to poke the base of Longarm's scrotum. "Let's do it the *really* dirty way, Custis. Hurry! Then I'll let you sleep."

Longarm woke the next morning with a hard-on. Imagine that. He looked down at his dong. It was a little red, but the sport last night on top of the rugged frolic of the night before had seemed to make it want even more.

Maybe those women really were demons. Maybe they'd cast some vicious sexual spell on him.

He took a whore's bath, staring out the window at the morning-bright street. He dressed in his freshly laundered clothes, and went downstairs to the dining room. Matilda blushed a little when, taking the order of three businessmen sitting at a table near the window, she turned toward him as he entered. Feigning nonchalance, she returned her attention to the three shopkeepers, then came over to where Longarm was sitting at a small table near the businessmen, with his own view of the street.

"You're up early," he said, keeping his voice down.

She looked around, cheeks mottling once more, and brushed a stray lock of hair from her eyes. "There's a funeral later this morning, and I got up to cook for the gathering at the Kelly house afterwards. Thought I might as well wait on a few tables."

"Funeral?"

"For Livvia Kelly's husband."

"Ah. What time?"

"Ten."

"Mmmm."

She frowned. "Are you going?"

Just to see her reaction, Longarm said, "Would it look inappropriate? I mean, since I didn't know the man. I'm tryin' to get a good look at all the womenfolk in town, and I figure nothin' attracts the womenfolk more than a funeral." He gave a wry snort. "Especially with coffee and cupcakes later."

"Well, I just think it seems a little odd, but I'm sure Livvia wouldn't mind."

Longarm dug a cheroot out of his shirt pocket. "How well do you know Mrs. Kelly?"

Mrs. Pringle canted her head slightly to one side. "You're interrogating me again."

"Am I?"

"You know you are." Her voice was huskier than

normal suddenly. Did that happen when she got her neck in a hump? "Why on earth . . ."

"I'm just the suspicious type," Longarm said, realizing that in this woman he'd really met his match. "Bring me whatever's good this mornin'. And a shot of . . ." He frowned. "What's that?"

"What?"

"That around your neck."

It was a gold locket studded with turquoise. She placed her hand over it, fingered it. "You mean this? It was my mother's. Has a little clock inside and a picture of her and my father." She stared at Longarm. "What's the matter?"

Yeah, what was the matter? He had a vague memory of one of the demon women wearing a gold locket. Had it been trimmed with turquoise? He was damn near certain it had been . . .

"Nothin'," he said as Matilda Pringle scrutinized him curiously, not looking a bit sheepish.

He watched her walk away, as puzzled as ever about who she truly was. If she was one of the Horsewomen of the Apocalypse, she was even more demonic than Whip Freeman could have imagined. If not, it was one hell of a coincidence that she looked and sounded so much like one of those kill-crazy females.

Not looking at him, she brought him a big, oval-shaped platter of ham, bacon, eggs, and fried potatoes, and set a thick stone mug of coal black coffee down beside it. He ate hungrily, planning his day. He'd go over and see the sawbones about the death of Jack Kelly, then after the funeral, he'd go over and talk to Mrs. Kelly herself.

It might not have been polite to talk to a woman

on the day of her husband's funeral, but something told Longarm she wouldn't be all that sad. If she was as good an actress as Mrs. Pringle, she'd look sad, all right. But he doubted that mourning would go any deeper than, say, the bite of a young mosquito.

If he had the brunette and the strawberry blonde accounted for here in Santa Clara, what about the other two demon women? Maybe, while waiting for the funeral and the following gathering at the Kelly house, he'd have a look around town, see if he could spy them. They might even be at the funeral and then later at the Kellys'—all trussed up in dowdy townswomen duds, with their hair pulled back to make them look like virgin schoolmarms.

Longarm snorted as he sipped his coffee.

He caught Mrs. Pringle staring at him from across the room, while setting breakfast platters down in front of four more customers. She turned away quickly, blushing again, fingering the gold locket, and headed back toward the kitchen.

Longarm took another sip of his coffee and stared at the swinging louver doors through which she'd disappeared, biting his mustache.

Chapter 15

"Liniment, Doc," Longarm said. "Liniment for my feet. Got stranded in the desert yesterday, and had to walk a tad farther than what even these low-heeled cavalry boots are good for. Do believe I raked a full layer of skin off. Every step I take now feels like I'm walkin' over burnin' coals, don't ya know!"

"What in the hell got you stranded out in the desert?"

Doctor Ambrose MacLeish was a tall man with a crooked jaw and one wandering eye. His office was over a furniture shop that doubled as an undertaking parlor, which to Longarm seemed a very practical setup all the way around. The pill roller turned around and waved the lawman inside his office, which still smelled of the bacon and biscuits he'd had for breakfast.

"I don't have a whole lotta secrets, Doc," Longarm said, kicking the door closed as he followed the man into his office. "But that one there I'll be takin' to the grave."

"That gets my imagination rolling."

"Let her roll."

The doctor had on a pair of wrinkled dress pants and a wrinkled white shirt, which he was just now tucking into his pants. Suspenders drooped at his thighs. His clodhopper shoes were worn but recently shined. "That all you come for—liniment?"

He turned away from Longarm to reach into a metal cabinet sitting behind a rolltop desk piled high with books and papers.

"I assume you're getting ready for Jack Kelly's funeral, so I won't keep you. I come to find out how he died."

"That's no big secret. Heart stroke. Didn't surprise me. His color was bad even in the summer. Sometimes shopkeepers, like doctors, don't get enough fresh air and exercise. *And* he was a teetotaler." MacLeish wagged his head disapprovingly as he handed a small glass jar to Longarm, and glanced at a low bench against the wall flanking the office door. "Sit down there. Take your boots off, and work that into your feet."

"Right here?"

"That's the only jar of that stuff I got. I'll just charge you a nickel for as much as you can work into your feet. If you want more, come back."

Longarm lifted the cap from the jar, and sniffed. "Smells like peppermint candy."

"Wintergreen. That'll take the fire out of your feet. I have an Indian gal who makes that and a few other things for me down on the Apache reservation. Go ahead. Call me a witch doctor. But those people often know more than we school-taught fellas do about what ails us mortals. Never seen the like."

Longarm sat down on the bench and began kicking

his boots off. The doctor stood tall and stoop-shouldered beside his desk, looping his suspenders up over his shoulders.

"Are you sure Kelly died of natural causes?" the lawman asked as he began peeling his right sock off his tender foot and wincing against the burning in his soles. "Any chance he could have been poisoned, say, but made to look like it was a heart attack?"

"I suppose that's possible, but from the coloration and the expression on the poor man's face—a big, wide-eyed death grin—I'd say it was a heart stroke. Who on earth would want to kill him anyway? He runs the only hardware store in town. Don't know what the ranch hands and miners are gonna do without him, unless Mrs. Kelly decides to keep the store open, run it herself."

"He didn't have any enemies?"

"None that I know of. He wasn't necessarily an easy man, but few men around this country are easy, Deputy Long. *Easy* men don't last long."

"Holy shit! That feels good," Longarm said with a relieved sigh as he rubbed the wintergreen balm into the sole of his right foot, massaging it between his toes from where dead skin hung in curls.

"Yeah, that'll cool you right off."

"What about his wife?"

The doctor had gone into another room that he apparently used for a bedroom, as Longarm could hear him opening and closing dresser drawers. "Are you asking me if she's easy?" The doctor chuckled. "Well, I couldn't tell you that, Marshal. I do know she came from Crossfire Valley, and you know what they say—"

"I have heard that about the Crossfire girls," Longarm said, removing his left sock. "But what I meant was . . ."

He let his voice trail off as he frowned down at the braided hemp rug beneath his feet. He looked toward the open door of the room in which the doctor was milling about, dressing for the funeral. "Mrs. Kelly's from Crossfire Valley, eh?"

"That's right. Quite a few around here are." The doctor appeared in the doorway.

He had a coat on, and his thick mop of gray hair was wet, showing the deep grooves of a careful combing. The oily smell of his origanum and bay rum tonic filled the room, nearly causing Longarm to choke.

The sawbones pressed his palms to his temples, soaking up some of the tonic, and continued: "The Crossfire was the first area settled in this country, because of the Saber River running through it. When the Tres Pinos outfit rerouted the river through Massacre Creek, bringing water to the ranch as well as to Santa Clara, the valley dried up, making it nearly impossible to raise beef there anymore." He hiked a shoulder. "So some moved out, others moved to town. They didn't like it much, but what could they do against the Tres Pinos?"

Longarm thoughtfully rubbed the balm into the sole of his left foot, breathing deep with relief but also remembering that the girl named Angie, whom the Tres Pinos riders had supposedly raped, had hailed from Crossfire Valley.

Longarm decided to leave that hole unpegged for the moment. Rerouting rivers—water rights in general—was a messy business. Such actions had spawned land wars in the past. He glanced up at the doctor, who now sagged into the swivel chair behind his desk and was fishing around in a desk drawer. "You think there's any chance Mrs. Kelly might have killed her husband, Doc?"

The sawbones looked incredulous. "Why in thunder would she do that? Jack Kelly was Livvia's ticket out of the desert of Crossfire Valley. She came from English paupers! He put a roof over her head, food in her belly!"

"Was he rich?"

"Jack? Hell, no! Why, he told me just last week that some miners up in the Andirons wanted some dynamite, and he had to make 'em pay up before he put the order in to El Paso. Said that since all his customers been living on credit—all except for Bart Spicer and his boys out at the Tres Pinos, of course—he was having to live on credit, too."

MacLeish shook his head and pulled a bottle out of his desk drawer. "Jack—rich? I'll say he wasn't. You'd better have a drink, Marshal. Clear your head."

"He have anything to do with rerouting the Saber River into Massacre Creek?"

The doctor frowned, shook his head. "I doubt it. That was mainly Spicer and his men who did that. His company paid for the rights at the land office here in Santa Clara, so it should have been all legal-like. The Crossfire farmers had ample opportunity to pay for some of that water, but they couldn't afford it." The frown lines in his age-spotted forehead deepened. "Say, what're you getting at?"

"I have no idea."

Longarm had finished pulling his socks on over the soothing wintergreen balm, and now he grabbed a boot. The doctor rummaged around for a couple of glasses, finding a water glass and a cracked green goblet, and splashed a couple fingers of whiskey into each.

Longarm didn't tell the doctor about seeing Mrs. Kelly over at the bank yesterday, only a day after her husband had died. He didn't want to start any rumors in case he was wrong about the woman, and he was beginning to have doubts that Mrs. Kelly was one of the demon women, just as there were more than a few seeds of doubt in his head about Mrs. Pringle. Neither woman seemed to have much motivation for riding roughshod across the Santa Clara basin. In Mrs. Kelly's case, that would have been like biting the hand that fed her.

Longarm got up and retrieved his drink from the doctor's desk, glancing down at his feet. "Damn, if that don't feel like a winter rich blowing on the soles of my poor feet!"

"I told ya you'd like it."

"Here's a silver dollar." Longarm dropped the coin on one of the many piles of sundry books, pamphlets, and papers on the doctor's desk. "Keep the change."

He sipped the cheap but bracing bourbon and looked out a window near the desk. "What about Mrs. Pringle, Doc. Know anything untoward about her?"

"Can't say as I do. Has always treated me kindly. The usual female complaints though she's been plagued with headaches from time to time."

"She ain't a Crossfire Valley girl, is she?"

"You know, Marshal, I don't know where she's from. Could be Crossfire though something tells me New Mexico. I do know she's righty purty, though I will say that Madison Pringle doesn't treat her all that well. He has a penchant for gambling, doesn't spend much time at home, and tends to leave his hotel chores to her. The headaches . . ."

The doctor let his voice trail off as he studied his glance, apparently having second thoughts about what he was going to say.

"I'll keep it in the family, Doc."

The sawbones threw back half of his bourbon, rubbed a forearm across his clean-shaven mouth. "I think her headaches might be . . . well, uh . . . pent-up energy, if you get my drift." He winked and grinned, the bourbon making his eyes bright.

Longarm threw back the rest of his own drink, stifling a snort. He set his glass on the desk. "Wouldn't doubt it a bit. Too bad someone man enough don't give her a roll now and then." He donned his hat and headed for the door. "I'll see you later, Doc."

"Stop by if your feet keep burning." The doctor tossed the coin in the air. "This is the first cash payment I've had in a month of Sundays. I get so sick of chicken I could cry."

Longarm pinched his hat brim to the man and went out.

He got to the bank too late to catch Whitehurst, who'd just left to attend Jack Kelly's funeral in the white church at the town's far western end. Quite a few people appeared to be going, as closed signs shone in more than a few shop windows, the shopkeepers themselves strolling arm in arm with their wives up the main street of Santa Clara, heading for the church.

Loitering on a shaded boardwalk, Longarm spied Mr. and Mrs. Pringle heading in the same direction. She saw Longarm as she walked arm in arm with her husband. He pinched his hat brim, evoking that flush again in her pretty face as she snapped her head forward. Pringle's left arm was in a sling. He didn't see Longarm.

Longarm found a little cantina on the town's northern edge. The mud-walled, earthen-floored shack faced the cemetery, which was sprawled across a low knoll and enclosed by a picket fence that was badly in need of fresh paint. There was one lone cottonwood in the bone-yard; otherwise it was all greasewood and sage separating the wooden crosses and gravestones.

There was a fresh mound of dirt that Longarm figured was awaiting the coffin of Jack Kelly. Longarm ordered a beer and a tequila shot and slouched into a chair near the lone, fly-spotted front window that offered a good view of the boneyard as well as Kelly's grave. He'd finished the beer but was still nursing the tequila shot, slowly turning the glass with thumb and index finger on the plank table before him, when the mourners came along the street to his left.

There were several wagons and horseback riders. Mrs. Kelly rode in the first buggy of the troupe, which was driven by the preacher and which also carried a stubby little woman whom Longarm assumed was the preacher's wife, dressed all in black, with a black hat and a black veil. Mrs. Kelly rode without expression, jostling slightly between the preacher and the preacher's wife. Mrs. Kelly's rich, strawberry blonde hair was secured in a French braid behind her head. She wore a small black hat with a black net veil.

As the cemetery was not far from the church, most of the mourners walked along behind the preacher's buggy, all dressed in their Sunday finest, the menfolk shielding the women from the sun with black parasols.

As they all filed through the picket gate and on up Cemetery Hill, Longarm kept a close eye out for the other Horsewomen of the Apocalypse—especially the one with hair the color of ripe wheat, and the Mexican. Seeing neither as the stragglers made their way along the tan path between the graves to the fresh mound halfway up the hill, Longarm frowned and threw the last of his tequila back.

He waited for the graveside service to end, and when the crowd had dropped down the hill, and dispersed, he followed the stragglers over to a little clapboard house just west of the cemetery. The house had a rough, brushy yard with a painted picket fence around it. Behind was a horse stable connected by a small rail corral to a buggy shed, and a privy.

Longarm kept himself hidden behind a woodpile on the opposite side of the rutted street from the Kelly house, smelling the food emanating from the house's screen door, hearing the low rumble of conversation. He saw no one who looked anything close to the beauties he was looking for arrive or leave—aside from Matilda Pringle, of course.

Finally, knowing such events could stretch on for a while, he took a slow, pensive walk around town. He smoked a couple of cheroots, stopped for a beer to cut the West Texas heat.

When he saw the crowd from the funeral trickle back up the main street, including the preacher and the preacher's wife, with the shopkeepers and their wives heading back to their stores, horseback riders heading back to their town dwellings or into the country, Longarm headed back to the Kelly house. On his way, he met Mr. and Mrs. Pringle. He tipped his hat to the couple. She dropped her eyes, blushing, and continued on along the street with her husband, a tin casserole in her hands.

Pringle looked owly with his arm in the sling. No wonder his wife got headaches, the lawman mused.

Longarm surveyed the Kelly place from a street cor-

ner. When after ten minutes no one came out, he walked
up the yard, pushed through the gate in the picket fence,
and strolled along the gravel path to the front porch. He
felt caddish for interrupting the woman's mourning by
nosing around—but was she really mourning? Maybe,
inside, she was really celebrating. And what would she
and her cohorts be up to next?

If she'd already cleaned out her husband's bank ac-
count, she could be intending on pulling her picket
pin—maybe in the company of the other three she-
demons—and lighting out for the high and rocky. The
Mexican border was only a day's ride south; if they got
down there, they'd be gone for good and so would all
the money they'd stolen.

Longarm pulled open the screen door, raised his hand
to knock, and froze. He'd heard the clap of a door on the
other side of the house. Gently, he closed the screen door
and walked around the side of the house in time to see
the backside of a leggy female in men's trail garb—calico
blouse, blue denims, and brown leather chaps—disappear
around the corner of the stable.

Looking around to see if he was being watched, Longarm broke into a run on the balls of his boots, and
pressed his back against the back of the stable. Through
the stable wall he could hear the snorts and stomps of
a horse, someone milling around, making scraping and
thumping sounds. Finally, hinges squawked, and there
was the scrape of double-hung doors opening.

Longarm ran around to the rear of the building. Dust
sifted between the two open doors. The strawberry
blonde galloped off along a twisting path atop a rangy
piebald, heading west along the north edge of the town,
a pair of overstuffed saddlebags flopping behind her.

Longarm pushed his hat brim back off his forehead, and stared after the woman's jouncing figure. He'd figured she was up to something, and that she'd be up to even more soon. He just hadn't figured on *this* soon.

Was that money stuffed in her saddlebags?

He had the urgent feeling that if he didn't get after her now, she'd be gone for good.

Whipping around, he was glad to see another horse in the stable, poking its head over a stall partition about halfway down on the stable's west side. He ran into the stable, found a saddle and blanket in a small tack room, and threw both and a bridle onto the roan gelding, which sidestepped away from him suspiciously, nickering anxiously.

He wished to hell he had his rifle, but he'd left the long gun in his hotel room. The six-shooter in his cross-draw holster would have to suffice.

He led the reluctant horse out of the stable, swung up into the saddle, and ground his heels into the gelding's flanks.

"Hee-yaahhhh!"

Chapter 16

It didn't take him long to catch up to the strawberry blonde. He rounded the shoulder of a bluff a half-mile west of Santa Clara, following her fresh tracks along a faint horse trail that had likely been a Comanche hunting trail at one time, and there she was, trotting her pie along a rocky flat.

He stayed well back of her, not wanting her to know he was following her. She rode with such purpose, never glancing behind, that he figured she was flying the proverbial Santa Clara coup and meeting up with the other three demon women somewhere along the trail. Hope rose in him. But wary of another ambush, he kept a sharp eye on his backtrail as well as on the escarpments and washes that rose and fell around him.

He wished to hell he had his Winchester.

She took a trail fork northward and it wasn't long before, riding about a quarter-mile behind his quarry, Longarm passed a weathered wooden sign announcing TRES PINOS LAND AND CATTLE COMPANY, LTD. He started

spying cattle grazing or lying in the shade of the widely
scattered alders and mesquites. Twenty or thirty of the
beeves lounged in the shade of a copse of alders along
what Longarm assumed was Massacre Creek, which
wound along the southern edge of Santa Clara, near the
railroad tracks.

The woman's trail followed the creek upstream, twisting and turning around stone outcroppings as it rose
higher into the broken, rocky, agave-studded foothills of
the Guadalupes. Longarm mounted a low ridge, and
reined up suddenly then turned the horse back behind a
thumb of rock extending out over the ridge.

Dismounting, he tied the horse to a piñon shrub, then
dropped to a knee to peer out around the thumb of the
outcropping.

The strawberry blonde had halted her horse near a
small stone, brush-roofed shack hunched in the deep
shade of a boulder-strewn slope that formed an easy arc
to the west and north of the hut—likely an old miner's
shack. The creek's fast-flowing water ran down toward
Longarm along the base of this boulder-strewn slope to
pass in front of him along the base of the ridge before
flowing on down into the desert flats where Santa Clara
was nestled.

Longarm watched the woman dismount in front of
the shack. She grabbed her saddlebags off the pie's back,
and walked up to the hovel. She dug into a pocket for
something, probably a key, then fiddled with the large
padlock hanging from a hasp on the door. He could hear
the clang of the lock as it fell free of the hasp, and the
faint squawk of the door when she nudged it open with a
boot toe.

She went into the shack then reappeared a couple of

minutes later without the saddlebags. She locked the door, mounted up, then swung her horse down the slope behind the shack and disappeared, only her tan dust rising in the sunlight behind her. The clatter of the buckskin's hooves dwindled.

Longarm stared down at the shack. He wanted to get a look at what was in those saddlebags, but couldn't risk losing the woman. Untying the roan's reins, he swung up into the saddle and put the horse down the rocky slope to the front of the shack.

He looked around carefully, making sure he wasn't riding into a trap, then followed the woman's trail around behind the shack and then down a steep slope that ran around behind the high ridge of boulders into a canyon on the ridge's other side.

At the bottom of the canyon, Longarm halted the roan, and looked around. The canyon bottom appeared to be a river bottom. The banks were lined with green willows and manzanita grass. The flora looked too lush along the banks for the river that had fed and nurtured it to have been dead for very long.

Longarm looked up at the large slope of boulders that had apparently tumbled down from the high sandstone ridge shouldering back against the western sky. He realized suddenly that what he was looking at wasn't the result of a mere rockslide but a planned dam. The boulders had likely been dynamited down from the lip of the western cliff and across the canyon of the river that had once flowed here.

It had rerouted the river water into the bed of what was now the very wet Massacre Creek, essentially killing the river and feeding water to the creek, which had probably run dry for most of the year before the dam.

Now the creek provided water not only for the broad valley housing the Tres Pinos spread but for the town of Santa Clara, as well.

If Longarm hadn't been confused enough by the do- ings of the Horsewomen of the Apocalypse, he sure as hell was now. Brows mantled curiously, wondering just what in the hell he was riding into, he put the roan down the dry course of the dead river.

Heat from the throbbing brass ball of the sun ham- mered him. The raspy squawks of hunting hawks echoed around him. Cicadas buzzed. The prints of the woman's horse marked the occasional stretches of alluvial sand and loam running down the middle of the canyon floor.

Occasionally as he rode, glancing cautiously at the stone and clay formations shifting around him, he spied a black-tailed rattler sunning itself on the riverbank or slithering between cracks along the pitted canyon walls.

The walls themselves rose and fell on either side of him as the canyon traced a meandering course through this rough, broken country. Apprehension nipped at Longarm.

Because of the canyon's twisting course, he couldn't keep the strawberry blonde in sight and was liable to ride right up on her before learning she'd stopped. Judg- ing by the clean tracks she'd left, she wasn't far ahead. Also, the walls afforded a good vantage from which some rifleman—or rifle*woman*—could stage an ambush.

They could blow him out of his saddle before he even heard the shot.

Soon he came to a point where the southern wall of the canyon virtually disappeared, offering a clean view of the open desert rolling off toward Mexico. Here was where his quarry's tracks turned abruptly right, scoring the sand and clay of the low southern bank, following a trail marked by deer and mountain lions. She appeared to have ridden straight south from here; Longarm followed the pie's tracks until he was halfway up a gentle hill capped with rocks, agave, and ocotillo.

From somewhere ahead, the smell of a cook fire tinged the dry breeze.

Dismounting, the lawman tied the horse to a shrub and climbed the hill, crouching, holding his .44 out from his belly. At the crest of the hill, he doffed his hat and hunkered down behind a flat-topped boulder before edging a look out around its left side.

Down the other side of the hill lay what appeared a jackleg ranch operation. There was a mud shack to the left, about sixty yards out from the base of the hill. It was surrounded by low, dun-colored bluffs bristling with prickly pear and Spanish bayonet.

To the right of the shack lay a two-story hay barn connected to a stable by a corral built from ocotillo branches. Behind the main corral lay a circular, stone-walled corral—a breaking corral, outfitted with a snubbing post. There was one horse inside the breaking corral, four inside the main corral.

Smoke issued from the adobe brick chimney of the long, low mud shack, which boasted a gallery propped on short stone pilings. The gallery was roofed with mesquite poles. An *ojo*—a clay water pitcher shaped like a bell—hung from the gallery rafters. There was an iron triangle on the front wall of the hut, beside a wooden ladle for the *ojo*.

A tall, hatless, stoop-shouldered man stood on the gallery, mopping the back of his neck with a red neckerchief. He was staring toward the stable. There was no one else in the yard, although the stable doors stood wide. Longarm waited, hunched down behind the boulder. When a figure appeared from between the doors, he jerked his head back behind the boulder then edged another look out from behind it again.

The strawberry blonde was closing the doors. The man on the gallery was speaking to her. Longarm could hear the man's voice, but he was too far away to make out what the man was saying.

His tone was sharp, angry, and he was jutting his pointed chin toward the girl, like a wedge. The strawberry blonde slumped toward him, slapping her hat against her chaps, causing dust to billow. She mounted the porch, tossed her hat on a low table, and dippered water from the *ojo*. She yelled something back at the tall man, who wore ragged work clothes and suspenders. A minute later, they both went inside the cabin, keeping the shack's door propped open with a brick, letting the cooling, early-evening air inside.

Longarm sank back against the boulder.

Was this the lair in which the four demon bitches holed up when they weren't out pillaging and plundering the county, and driving men like Whip Freeman—not to mention Longarm *himself*—mad?

If so, where were the other three? Likely headed this way. Maybe all Longarm had to do to corral the four and their obvious cohorts in the cabin was wait.

As long as the woman he'd followed out here, Mrs. Kelly, really was one of the Four Horsewomen of the Apocalypse. Did he really know for sure? The best way to find out was probably to scamper on down to the cabin and listen through the walls. Surely, if she and the man inside thought they were alone, Longarm would hear some incriminating information.

He glanced at the western sky. The sun was still about an hour above the horizon. There was a lot of open ground between his perch and the cabin. He'd wait until the huge orange balloon had at last fallen behind the western ridges before he'd tramp on down the hill and into the yard, lest he should be seen and possibly shot from one of the windows.

After a time, he walked down the north slope toward the river bottom, slipped the bit from the roan's mouth, and loosened its saddle cinch. He'd likely be here awhile and he wanted the horse to rest comfortably and be ready to ride again when he needed it.

He went back up to the ridge crest, sat down against the boulder, tested the wind with a wet finger, and lit a cheroot. He'd smoked the cigar halfway down when he heard the distant thuds of galloping hooves from the direction of the cabin. Mashing the cigar into the ground, he whipped around and peered down the side of the hill. The sun was almost down, burnishing the desert, limning the rocks and sparse foliage in charcoal shadows.

A single rider approached the ranch yard from the south, heading straight toward Longarm and silhouetted against the sand-colored sky. Golden dust puffed around the horse's hooves—a dun with a white neck and breast. The slender rider wore man's trail clothes; long, wheat blond hair flopped across her shoulders.

Longarm's heart thudded.

The wheat blonde rode into the yard. A female voice hailed the cabin, and then the rider swung the dun over toward the corral, and dismounted. Quickly, the woman unsaddled the mount, set her tack on a top rail, turned the horse into the corral, and tramped toward the house. Longarm could hear her spurs chinging.

The tall man stepped out of the cabin, said something to the girl while flexing his suspenders with his thumbs. She said something to the man then mounted the gallery and followed him on into the cabin.

Behind Longarm, more hooves thudded. These came from the river bottom, which he'd followed down canyon from the dam.

He scrambled on all fours about six feet down the ridge then scurried over to the roan, which was getting ready to lift a startled whinny, when Longarm clamped his hand over the horse's nostrils. Wrapping his other arm around the gelding's neck, he chomped down on one ear and wrestled the indignant beast to the ground and held it there, gritting his teeth anxiously.

The thuds grew louder. He heard the rattle of a bridle bit. The sounds came from about twenty yards east along the side of the ridge.

As he held the horse, slumped over the befuddled beast's head, he saw the horse and rider move straight up from the river bottom. There was enough light left that he could see the broad-chested Appaloosa the woman straddled.

The sun limned Matilda Pringle's billowy cream blouse and knotted red neckerchief in golden-brown hues. Below the neckerchief, the gold, turquoise-studded locket flopped.

Her broad hat brim shaded her eyes, chestnut hair curling down her back. She rode straight up and over the ridge, looking neither to her right nor left, kicking rocks loose as she and the big Appy descended the opposite slope, heading for the ranch yard.

As the hoof thuds dwindled, Longarm released the horse's ear and snout, and heaved a deep sigh of relief.

He rolled away from the horse, and the big beast regained its feet heavily, blowing hard and angrily. Longarm stood, as well, brushing himself off and wondering what gods were fond enough of him to have kept the woman from following his and Mrs. Kelly's tracks up from the river bottom, and riding right up on him and the roan.

He walked back up to the top of the ridge and took his place again behind the boulder, edging another careful look into the ranch yard. The brunette, whom he figured to be Mrs. Pringle with incredibly good acting skills, had just turned her own horse into the stable. The big Appaloosa was down on the ground and churning up an enormous cloud of salmon-colored dust as it rolled and kicked.

The woman was striding purposefully toward the cabin. The two blondes, hatless, were on the porch, facing her and speaking. He could hear the trill of their female voices but couldn't make out what they were saying.

He saw the fourth she-demon before they did, galloping toward the ranch yard from the southeast, coming at an angle ahead of a safflower dust swirl. This one wore black and red. Most of her attire matched the black braid pulled forward over her right shoulder to flop down her well-filled, bloodred blouse and black brush jacket.

The señorita.

In a few minutes, they were all in the cabin together.

Longarm watched lamplight glow in the windows, growing brighter as the sun died. The smells wafting from the chimney made his mouth water and his stomach growl. Coyotes yammered in the hills around him. Somewhere in the far distance, a bobcat snarled.

When it was dark enough that he figured he wouldn't be seen from the shack, he headed on down the slope, moving at a crouch, the Colt extended in his right hand. The smells of wood smoke and roast venison grew, and threads of smoke wafted around him as he closed the gap between the base of the ridge and the cabin. He tried to stay out of sight of the horses in the corral, as one of the mounts might nicker or whinny, and give him away.

He pressed his back to the cabin wall.

Through the mud bricks behind him, he could hear the low murmur of sporadic conversation, pans clattering, the muted thuds of boots on an earthen floor. The old man said something that Longarm couldn't quite make out.

"Goddamn it, Pa," one of the girls said sharply. "How many fuckin' times I gotta tell you—I couldn't stand that man gruntin' around between my legs no longer!"

"Did ya have to kill him, Livvie?" one of the other girls said. "It's too damn early. We weren't done raisin' a ruckus yet! Haven't even burned old Bart Spicer outta that fancy lodge o' his!"

"With that lawman skulkin' around—as fine a piece a horseflesh as he may be," snickered the raspy-voiced brunette, "it was probably just as well little Livvie went ahead and screwed old Kelly into an early grave. Now we can go ahead and kill the rest . . . startin' with the town council."

The girls laughed. The old man growled, muttered reprovingly.

"What about the lawdog?" asked the old man.

"Well, I reckon we kill him."

"When? Where we gonna find him?"

Gravel crunched faintly to Longarm's right. He saw a shadow move.

Hot blood surged in his ears. It surged again when he heard a hammer cock, saw the black-and-red-clad figure of the señorita step up beside him and press a short-barreled .36 revolver against his temple. "I know where," she said menacingly in her Spanish-accented English. "Right here!"

Above Longarm's head, a wooden shutter flew open. Three more pistols were extended toward him, angled down toward the top of his head.

He raised his eyes to see over his brows the three maws yawning down at him. Above the guns hovered the smiling faces of the three other Horsewomen of the Apocalypse.

"Ah, shit," Longarm said.

Chapter 17

"Try anything, ya lawdogging bastard, an' I'll cut you in two with *this*!"

The man's voice had come from behind Longarm. The lawman turned his head to see the tall, stoop-shouldered gent standing at the corner of the mud shack, aiming a long, double-barreled shotgun at Longarm's head.

The guns dangling out the window disappeared, and Longarm could then hear the thuds of boots and the raucous ringing of spurs as the three girls scrambled toward the shack's front door. Longarm shifted his gaze from the beautiful señorita, whose red shirt and silver trimmings flashed in the starlight, to the hatless, stoop-shouldered man holding the shotgun on him.

It was good and dark, so Longarm couldn't make out much of his face aside from his nose, nearly as long a hatchet handle, against the starry western sky. He had a thin neck, and he spoke in a faint English accent.

"Toss that hogleg out here," he croaked. "Real slow.

Just two fingers. Any fast moves, I'll blow your law-doggin' head to a bloody pulp!"

Slowly, Longarm lifted the Colt Frontier in his right hand, using only his thumb and index finger. He tossed it away. It landed in the dust with a thud similar to the one the stone had made falling in his gut.

His thoughts immediately turned to the double-barreled derringer in his vest pocket, attached to his old railroad watch nestling in the opposite pocket by a gold-washed chain. Could he get to it before these killers found it? With only two barrels, it likely wouldn't matter much if he did.

"Get up—*vete*!" said the señorita, kicking Longarm's right hip and holding her own cocked Smith & Wesson on him. "Mr. Gentry is very handy with his Greener."

The three other girls came running, breathless, down the side of the shack. They fanned out behind the oldster with the shotgun, all three holding their pistols on Longarm.

"Ain't this sweet," Longarm said. "All five of us together again." He looked at the old man. "Gentry, huh?"

"Shut up!" intoned the strawberry blonde, stepping forward.

"What's he mean—'again'?" said the old man, frowning at the strawberry blonde, whom Longarm took to be his daughter. "What's he mean by that, Livvie?"

Longarm snorted. "Didn't they tell you we—"

"Livvie told you to shut up!" said the brunette.

Longarm still couldn't tell if she was Matilda Pringle or not. Try as he did to scrutinize her face, he couldn't see her very well in the inky desert darkness. She had to be. There were too many other physical similarities. It was her personality that didn't fit . . .

"Livvie, huh?" Longarm looked from the brunette to the other three. "I reckon I might as well know all your names—don't you think? Since we've become such pals an' all, and I been a might curious, as you'd expect."

"Pals?" croaked the old man, frowning and looking around at the deadly women. "I still don't know what he's talkin' about. You girls meet up with him before?"

"You could say that," Longarm said.

"It's a long story, Pa," said the former Olivia Gentry, sneering at Longarm. "Too long for us to go into here. We got a long night ahead. Go ahead an' kill him. We'll toss him into the ravine yonder. Wildcats gotta eat, too."

"No, no, no," snarled the old man, keeping the shotgun aimed at Longarm's head. "That's too damn easy for this scum-sucking lawdog comin' snoopin' around, sidin' with that devil town and them Tres Pinos bastards."

"What do you suggest?" said the blonder of the blondes. She also had the highest voice; with the hardness she gave it now, it sounded weird, doubly menacing. "If we don't kill him, we've worked hard these past two years for nothing."

"We let him die slow." Gentry looked at his daughter standing to his left. "Livvie, fetch some rope. We're gonna throw his lawdoggin' ass into the mine shaft. Give him to them black-tailed rattlers down there. They'll know what to do with him." His snaggly, tobacco-stained teeth flashed as he grinned. "They'll hear his howls as far away as Santa Clara."

"You sure this is wise?" asked the señorita.

She was staring at Longarm, dark eyes glistening in the starlight. Her breasts rose and fell heavily behind the red shirt and black vest; so did those of the other two girls standing around the old man.

Longarm could hear their excited breathing. They were crazy. To a girl, they were plum loonier than a tree full of owls. Torturing, killing, fucking—it was all the same to the Four Horsewomen of the Apocalypse.

"We got time yet. Don't wanna get over to Tres Pinos before midnight anyways. Need to surprise 'em. Hell, we got a good hour before we need to set out. What the hell else we gonna do to chew up the time?"

The old man gritted his teeth. "Me—I grew up with the great state o' Texas. Fought for it, in fact. No law-dog, includin' the Texas Rangers I once respected, ever sided with the folks of Crossfire Valley. For that, you're gonna die hard, you badge-totin' federal bastard."

"I reckon it's gettin' clear to me now," Longarm said. "Tres Pinos rerouted the river that once fed this valley and likely made your ranches viable operations. Now the river runs across Tres Pinos range and feeds Santa Clara. And that's what this little war is all about."

"War?" The wheat blonde snickered. "There ain't no war, lawdog. We're killin' an' stealin' at will. Anyone who stood against the folks of Crossfire Valley is fair game. 'Specially them privy snipes over to Tres Pinos. That outfit was misusin' the women and girls of the Crossfire Valley for years, even before they rerouted the river to dry us out."

Longarm said, "Yeah, I heard about Miss Angie. You ever think about leavin' that up to the law?"

"There ain't no law around here," said the brunette, who spoke with a rasp but whose English was far rougher and cruder than Mrs. Pringle's. It was only that which left the seed of doubt in the lawman's mind.

"There was until you shot him out of his saddle."

The brunette laughed huskily. The old man grinned.

The señorita toed a boot in the sand. Longarm had a feeling she was blushing, proud.

"Alden Anderson wouldn't have lifted a hand against those men," said the man with the shotgun. "Tres Pinos owned him just like they own everyone else in the town. To make themselves feel better about assaultin' our women, they said they was easy. That they was whores!"

"So you married 'em off to the men of Santa Clara . . ." Longarm scowled through the darkness at the man. He was utterly baffled.

"That was my idea." This from Livvie Gentry Kelly, who came around the rear corner of the shack, a three-foot length of rope in her hand. She chuckled. "I told it to Pa, an' he went along."

"Not at first, I didn't. Couldn't see no daughter of my own marryin' up with them Santa Clara rubes, but after I got to thinkin' on it, I thought—my, what sweet revenge!"

He hooded his deep-set eyes and wagged the shotgun at Longarm. "Get down on your belly. My daughter's gonna tie your hands behind your back. You make one move against her, and I'll do like Livvie says and blow your head clean off your shoulders." He grinned again. "We're gonna take us a little walk over to your final restin' place."

Longarm glanced at the eyes glittering in kill-crazy delight around them. Finally, he dropped to his hands and knees then pressed his belly flat against the ground. Quickly, adeptly, Livvie tied his wrists behind his back.

"Might as well tell me your names, ladies." Longarm lifted his chin. "Why the hell not? I'm gonna be dead soon anyway."

"You know Livvie," said the old man. He glanced at

the señorita. "This is the daughter of a dear friend of mine, dead too soon—killed, in fact, by Bart Spicer's men, who said he was rustling. "She is Bibi Velasco. Married up with the banker, Whitehurst, don't ya know!"

"*Sí*," said Bibi, grinning. "He works late every night, counting his money, which made it easier for me to . . . how do you say? . . . run roughshod around Santa Clara with *mis amigas*."

"Whitehurst," Longarm said, his voice betraying his amazement. "How come you weren't at the funeral?"

"He didn't like me to leave the house." Bibi stuck her breasts out. "Afraid I would drive the other men crazy." She laughed wickedly. "And he thought I obeyed his every order—staying at home and cleaning his house for him every minute of every day and night!"

Gentry turned to the wheat blonde. "Emma Peeters's family is still in the valley, barely holding on. Soon the water will return, and they'll be able to grow wheat and cattle again."

Longarm had already turned to the brunette before the old man said, "And last but not least of the soldiers in my small but deadly army is Queenie Walters. Her father raised her and three sisters down at the other end of the valley. Her family is dead . . . all but one sister."

"You might have met her in town," said Queenie. "She looks like me—only, she lacks my guts. You see, she *willingly* married that old faker and cowering fool, Pringle. She was yellow-livered, too. Jumped sides and legitimately married a townsman when she saw who was winning."

The brunette shook her head and curled her upper lip. "Don't worry—I'll be killing her husband at sunup tomorrow, along with my own and the rest of the men in Santa Clara. Eventually, Matilda will thank me."

"Like to humiliate 'em first, eh?" Longarm growled, glancing back at the old man's daughter. "Or . . . fuck 'em to death!"

"What's that he said?" Gentry said, cupping a hand to his ear before turning to his daughter. "Did he say what I thought he said?"

"He only means ole Jack, Pa." She giggled. "I figured that'd be the best way I could avoid suspicion before I lit outta town."

The old man stared, mouth agape, at his daughter. Then his eyes lowered to her heaving bosom, her blouse open to reveal four inches of her deep, tan cleavage. His shoulders jerked as he laughed. "Child," he said, running the back of his hand across her cheek adoringly, "ain't you a caution?"

"All right, Papa," Livvie cajoled the old man play-fully, sweeping her hair back from her face coquettishly. "Keep it in your pants!"

"We best get this show on the road," said Queenie Walters, prodding Longarm's ribs with her boot toe. "Get up, lawdog. Time for that last, long walk. Soon, you'll be snugglin' with the snakes—right where you belong."

Longarm rose awkwardly. His derringer was still in his vest pocket. It wasn't doing him much good there at the moment, however. He couldn't have gotten his hands on it if he'd wanted to do.

"You'd best lead the way, Pa," said Livvie Gentry. "I don't remember the way, and it's getting' so darn dark, I'd probably tumble right into it."

"All right." The old man lowered his shotgun and began walking eastward along the back of the shack. "Bring him along, girls. Keep your guns on him. If he tries to run, wing him." He chuckled as he headed off east of the shack. "Wing him good. Make him howl!"

He chuckled again. One of the women poked a gun barrel against Longarm's back.

The lawman started walking. Dread filled him. He'd been up against it before, but he was really up against it now. These four kill-crazy beauties were every bit as deadly as any male outlaw he'd ever tracked. Their beauty was intoxicating. Even now he felt a vague pull below his belly. Maybe it was their disarming allure that had caused him to get reckless and walk right into their trap.

Obviously, the brunette had seen his tracks, maybe even seen him and the roan perched atop the northern ridge . . .

"Tell me somethin' else," he said as he followed the old man east across the desert, meandering around prickly pear and agave patches. "What was Grogan Caulfield's part in all this?"

"Oh, that old reprobate," scoffed the wheat blonde, Emma. "He worked for Pa. He was in town pickin' up supplies at the mercantile. Can't say as I know what got into his head, but I reckon he wanted to be our hero—as if we needed one . . ."

"Always did wanna get in my pants," laughed Livvie.

"For what it's worth," said Matilda Pringle's sister behind Longarm, keeping her raspy voice low so the hard-of-hearing old man wouldn't hear, "I'm glad you drilled him. Otherwise, we wouldn't have gotten to know each other."

She prodded his back jeeringly with her gun barrel. Longarm cursed as he stumbled forward. The back of his neck burned with chagrin.

Following the old man and flanked by the four beautiful demons, he climbed a hill that grew gradually steeper. Boulders jutted here and there among the spindly shrubs and sotol that slanted like long witch's fingers against the velvet, starry sky.

When the group came to the top of the ridge, the old man slowed his pace.

"Dang," he grumbled, "can't see the damn hole so good at night. Been a while since I been up here."

He moved forward. Longarm could hear his raspy breathing.

"It should be right ahead of you, Pa," said Livvie directly behind Longarm.

The lawman stopped and looked around. There was a dark splotch in a slight hollow just ahead of the old man. Ahead and right of Longarm was dense darkness, as though a canyon opened there. Longarm didn't have to think about his next move.

As the old man took mincing steps forward, swinging his head back and forth, Livvie said, "Careful now, Pa . . ."

Longarm bounded forward, slammed his left shoulder into the old man's right side. The old man and Livvie screamed at the same time. The old man flew forward into the black rug on the ground that was the mouth of the mineshaft he'd been looking for. His screams echoed woodenly from underground.

At the same time, Longarm dashed to his right and bounded off his boot heels, diving over the lip of the ridge and into the darkness stretching like a broad black field ahead of him.

Behind, pistols kicked up a wicked thunder.

"Drill the bastard!" shouted the raspy-voiced brunette.

Chapter 18

As Longarm hit the slope and began rolling, he heard the old man's hollow screams echo from inside the grave that he and the girls had meant for the hand-bound lawman.

Shrilly, Livvie screamed, "Pa! Pa!"

Knowing that he could very well be committing suicide as opposed to being murdered, Longarm rolled on down the steep slope. He couldn't have slowed his tumble if he'd wanted to.

He had no idea how deep a canyon he'd thrown himself down, or what obstacles he'd run into—for all he knew he'd impale himself on a ocotillo or tumble into another mine shaft. All he could do was pray for a soft landing and hope that the slugs pinging and spanging around him didn't hit their target.

The bullets screeched and thudded, trimming shrub branches and kicking up sand and gravel.

Longarm rolled, feeling sharp rocks poking and prodding him. Twice he bounced off the sides of boulders.

He flew straight over a piñon that grabbed at his boots
and caused him to roll ass over teakettle. He heard himself grunting and groaning with every impact.

When he finally piled up on flat ground—the sudden
concussion hammering the breath from his lungs with
a loud *woosh!*—he thought for a moment that having
rolled like that, with his hands tied behind his back,
he might have dislocated both shoulders. They felt as
though a long, rusty lance had been driven from one to
the other.

The pistols continued to pop but they sounded much
farther away now. The bullets thumped and spanged
several yards above the ravine bottom he'd landed in. As
he lifted his head, snarling and cursing like a wounded
bobcat, he saw the occasional pinprick flash of a pistol a
good sixty or seventy yards above him and through a
silhouetted mesh of rocks and shrubs.

A thumb of rock poked out from the bank just ahead.
Digging his heels into the gravel, he pushed himself
backward behind the knob and well out of range of the
girls continuing to shoot at him sporadically from the
ridge. He could hear them yelling among themselves,
their attention obviously diverted from him to the old
man in the hole, which was exactly what Longarm had
intended.

The lawman looked around. He needed a sharp rock
to cut the rope binding his wrists together. Finding nothing here, he looked up and down the wash. Nothing there
either. At least, nothing that he could see in the darkness.

He remembered the peashooter in his vest pocket. As
he looked down at his sand-covered vest, another stone
dropped down the deep, empty well of his belly. The gold-
washed chain was gone. He'd lost it in the tumble down

the hill—watch, chain, and the double-barreled derringer he might have used to shoot through the rope.

"Shit!"

Rocks tumbled down the ridge, following the same path he'd taken a moment before. He could hear a girl grunting. More rocks and sand clattered down the slope to thud and sift onto the ravine floor a few yards away.

One of the she-devils was coming down the ridge.

Longarm heaved himself onto his knees, stretched his lips back from his teeth as he pushed to his feet, feeling as though every joint in his body had been badly wrenched. Even his chin was skinned and burning; he could feel the coolness of blood mixed with the sand.

He was glad nothing was broken, or seemed broken. With all the electricity coursing through him, he might not know the full extent of his injuries for several hours.

Continuing to hear someone moving down the ridge, Longarm broke into a run along the ravine floor where it curved eastward between high, rocky banks. There was just enough starlight for making out the major obstacles in his path, but not enough for the smaller ones. He tripped twice over driftwood mesquite, once over a rock hidden by the shadow of a prickly pear patch, and fell hard.

After the last fall, he paused on one knee, raking air in and out of his lungs. The air was still, quiet. Atop the ridge from which he'd flung himself he could hear a girl sobbing. That would be Livvie.

Her old man must have bought the farm. Too damn bad Longarm couldn't have made sure his daughter and all the rest of the she-bitches had joined him.

He could sympathize with their plight—the wealthy landowner against the smaller ones. But what they'd

been doing in this country had gone far and above what
any man—or woman—could rightfully call justifiable
revenge. They'd become every bit as bad or worse than
the men they'd been fighting. Like a pack of rabid curs,
they needed to be put down.

"Tough intentions for a man who'd damn near been
fucked to death by 'em and who's now runnin' for his
life *from* 'em," he growled, glancing back the way he'd
come.

Two shadows moved behind him. He heard mutter-
ing, the rattle of a kicked stone.

Grunting as he heaved himself off a battered knee, he
continued running forward, wishing like hell he could
free his hands. A gun cracked. The last thing Longarm
heard was the spang of the bullet off the rock wall to his
right. The last thing he felt was an angry nip in his right
temple.

Then everything went black.

Silence engulfed him until, gradually, the vacuum was
penetrated by an unidentifiable sound. As the sound grew
louder, he identified it as a slurping sound.

The slurping continued to grow in volume until it
seemed to beckon Longarm up from the deep pit of un-
consciousness he'd languished in. A warmth registered
on his eyelids. Something damp pressed against his back
and his butt.

He opened his eyes, heard himself groan as morning
sunlight poured into his eyes like a fistful of thrown
thorns. He blinked. His shoulders felt as though they'd
been partly pulled from their sockets. He groaned again,
and the slurping sound died abruptly.

Through squinted eyes he saw a creature standing

some distance away, to his right. The dun-and-gray coyote stood with its head down, front feet spread, staring back at Longarm down the long, clean line of its whiskered snout.

The beast was obscured by a webbing of brush that scraped lightly against Longarm's face. Slowly, keeping its brown eyes on the lawman, the coyote lowered its head once more and lapped up water with its tongue.

Water...

Longarm looked around. He lay in a shallow trough on one side of the riverbed along which he'd been running when the girls had pinked him with a ricochet. There was water in the trough.

Gently swirling water was washing down the riverbed to his right, seeping into the trough beneath him. The water flashed in the morning sunlight, hammering the lawman's retinas and causing his head to pound almost as severely as it had pounded from the hangover the poisoned spring had given him.

He could feel the burn of the graze across his right temple, and the dried blood. He had no way of knowing, but it didn't seem overly bad. Just painful.

Probably just rattled his brains around some.

He lifted his head. The coyote lifted its own head abruptly, made a mewling sound, then wheeled and splashed along the edge of the shallow stream and scampered up a dusty draw and out of sight.

Longarm tried to sit up. His shoulder and his bullet-grazed head rebelled, the pain so bad that it almost made him pass out. He couldn't feel his hands; they were still tied behind him. He could tell he was lying on them by the pain in his shoulder and by the bulge in his lower back.

"Christalmighty!" he fairly screamed as he forced himself over onto his right shoulder and then continued rolling, hearing the brambles thrash as he rolled through them, until he lay belly down on the wet floor of the riverbed.

Futilely, he fought the ropes lashing his numb wrists together. As he did so, he stared at the brown water swirling around him and making a very faint trickling sound as it slid over the rocks and flailed gently against the ridges on either side of the narrow canyon.

Last night, the canyon had been dry.

It dawned on him what had happened.

The girls, with or without the old man whom Long-arm had pushed into the mineshaft, had blown the damn and rerouted the river back to its original course. They likely hadn't known whether they'd shot him or not, since he'd fallen into the trough screened with brush, and it had been nearly as dark as the inside of a glove.

"The Good Lord watches over fools an' children, as my ole ma used to say," he muttered now, lifting his chin above the swirling water and again trying to free his numb hands and aching wrists. No doing. He had to find a sharp object. Or the derringer he'd dropped on the ridge during his tumble.

Grunting and groaning, feeling as though he'd spent a night in a torture chamber, he gained his knees and looked around warily, wondering if the women had returned to look for him after they'd blown the dam. He figured they could be back anytime; he had to move fast.

He heaved himself to his feet and retraced his steps from last night, splashing along the six or seven inches of moving water. He was lucky the river was low this time of the year, or he'd likely have drowned in the trough he'd rolled into.

The Good Lord watches over fools . . .

Last night, he hadn't made it far from the spot at which he'd tumbled down the ridge, and he had no trouble finding it now, wading in the river. He inspected the slope and ridge carefully, keeping his ears pricked for sounds of the women. Then he started climbing, picking his way carefully, digging his heels into the thin soil, bracing his feet against tufts of grass and against fixed rocks and boulders.

As he climbed slowly, weak from the bullet graze and all the scrapes and bruises he'd incurred in the fall, he scoured the slope for his derringer. He'd about give up on it when he saw the sun glinting off the gold chain curving out from under some freshly churned dirt.

Dropping to his knees, he grabbed the chain in his teeth, and heaved a relieved sigh when he saw the gun and the watch dangling in front of him. Of course, he couldn't use the derringer until he was relatively sure the shot wouldn't draw the girls. But at least he had two bullets, and that gave him a little comfort.

He continued on up the ridge, having to crawl on his knees, guns and watch dangling from his teeth. At the top, he collapsed and lay there, breathing hard, his lips flecked with dirt and sand. The derringer was on the ground near his face.

When he'd recovered some strength, he straightened his back, and looked around. The hole was only a few yards away, the ground around it scored by the girls' boots.

The ranch lay to his left and below the ridge, the

midmorning sun glaring down on the shack, barn, stable, and corral. There were no horses in the corral. He wasn't sure whether to feel happy or glad about that. No horses meant the girls likely weren't here. It also meant that, unless he could find the roan he'd swiped from the Kelly barn, he was stranded miles from town on foot.

He grabbed the derringer in his teeth and heaved himself to his feet. He stumbled over to the oblong hole at the mouth of the mineshaft, and looked down. The old man lay at the bottom, all piled up and crooked, chin dipped to a shoulder.

The double-bore shotgun lay beside him. Blood shone darkly beneath his head, which the sun striped with golden light.

Since he was still here, the girls were likely nowhere around. Obviously, the old man's death hadn't deterred them from following through with their plan to blow the dam. For that, Longarm was grateful.

Now, remembering their sinister vow to kill every man in Santa Clara, Longarm needed to run them to ground before they did any more damage. Obviously, easier said than done . . .

He sat down, dropped the derringer from his teeth. Squirming around, he picked up the gun with his right hand, clicked one of the two small hammers back, and pressed the nose of the peashooter against the rope, making sure he had it aimed toward the ground.

Pop!

Dirt and sand blew up around him.

He gave his wrists a light jerk, and the rope fell away. Slowly, he brought his hands back around in front of him, stretching his lips back from his teeth and arching his back as his shoulders rolled forward, grating like unoiled ball bearings, the blood surging back into his hands and igniting the nerve ends in his fingers.

At length, he stood, pocketed the peashooter, and began tramping down toward the ranch yard. If the Good Lord had seen fit to leave his six-shooter there, Longarm would become a churchgoing man. If He'd seen fit to leave the roan somewhere nearby, as well, he might even quit the lawdog business to become a monk . . .

Chapter 19

Longarm decided that the first thing he'd do when he returned to Denver was to partake of a church service, for he found his six-shooter about thirty feet behind the mud shack, where he'd tossed it the night before.

He did not have to worry about joining the monkhood, however. When he found the roan, there wasn't much left of the poor beast, besides the saddle and bridle, once the wildcats had finished with it. The dead horse was maybe what had attracted the coyote Longarm had discovered drinking from the stream, cutting the salty taste of the roan's blood.

The lawman cursed and, leaving the horse to the buzzards that had swarmed over it, with magpies and crows waiting in the branches of a droopy alder, headed on down the slope toward the riverbed. He washed his face and head in the cool water, took a long drink, and rising, winced at the prospect of walking a long distance again on feet that had not yet recovered from his previous long tramp across the desert.

Suppressing the discomfort not only of his feet but his grazed arm, grazed head, and sundry contusions and abrasions, he started off along a game path following the stream. After an hour's walking, stopping twice to bathe his burning feet in the cool water, he came to where the girls had blown the damn. It looked like a sacked castle, the river pouring over rocks and boulders where it had once been turned east to feed the Tres Pinos and Santa Clara.

Longarm walked on past the mine shack, where he now realized the old man's daughter had stashed the dynamite she'd taken from her husband's mercantile. Soon he was on the horse trail that would lead him, after a long tramp, to Santa Clara.

He was just beginning to wonder if he'd make it in a day, when, glancing north, he saw smoke rising from behind a low ridge. He spied something else—a moving figure—in the periphery of his vision, and turned to see a horseback rider moving toward him at a shambling trot. He unholstered his Colt, and waited, staring doubtfully at the approaching horse. Its rider rode hunched, the man's head nearly hidden by the horse's neck. Obviously, something was wrong.

Longarm stepped in front of the horse, and the beast stopped itself, the man in the saddle lifting his head with a start and narrowing pain-racked eyes at Longarm. He held a bloody arm across his bloody belly. He was a young man in his early twenties, with close-cropped blond hair and the sunburned face of a line rider.

"What the hell happened, boy?" Longarm asked, grimacing at the blood oozing from the belly wound and over the young man's arm.

The young drover groaned as he lowered his head

once more, and sagged toward Longarm. The lawman eased the boy out of the saddle, gentled him to the ground, where he lay on his back, grimacing and panting.

"Them she-devils," the drover croaked. "They burned the Tres Pinos!"

Longarm glanced at the horse, saw the three thumb-sized trees forming a triangle on the horse's right wither—the Tres Pinos brand.

"It was the boss's wife!" the young man said, shoulders jerking as pain racked him.

"Boss's wife?"

The kid nodded. "Mrs. Spicer. Here we all thought . . . she was so purty an' nice!"

Longarm put a hand on the obviously dying young man's shoulder and stared off at the smoke rising above the bald, rocky hill. "I bet you did, son," he said absently. "I bet you did."

So Emma Peeters had married Spicer. Longarm laughed, sleeved sweat from his brows. He had to hand it to the women—they sure knew how to take revenge on a bunch of fool men. They had it down to an art.

He looked down at the kid, was about to pull him into some shade. But there was no use. The young man had let his arms fall slack. His head had sagged back against the ground, his chest unmoving. His eyes had acquired a glassy stare straight into the sun above Longarm.

"Sorry, kid. You didn't deserve this."

Hardening his jaws in anger, he grabbed the dead younker under the arms and dragged him into the rocks beside the trail. No time to bury the lad. The Four Horsewomen of the Apocalypse were likely headed for Santa Clara to continue their mission.

He swung up onto the pinto cow pony's back, and batted his heels against its side, lurching off at a gallop eastward along the winding ranch trail.

Longarm saw the rooftops of the town rise before him a little over an hour later. Instantly, he knew something was wrong. Silence hovered over the town like a dark pall.

Usually, even when business was slow, you could hear the clang of a blacksmith's hammer or a mother calling to her children. Maybe a kid out splitting wood for the coming night's fire.

But now in the early afternoon, Santa Clara could have been a ghost town. Longarm crossed the muddy riverbed through which fresh water once ran. As he rode up on the town from the northwest, threading his way between outlying shacks and corrals, the only movement he could see was the wind spinning mini–dust devils and jostling tumbleweeds, a few goats and chickens milling in their respective pens.

Even the animals seemed subdued, shocked by some catastrophic event they were in the midst of but couldn't quite grasp.

Longarm reined up near a small adobe shack. A pale oval face appeared in a window of the shack, then quickly disappeared, a threadbare red curtain jostling where the face had been. The lawman swung down from the pinto's back, and slid the drover's saddle-ring Winchester carbine from the saddle boot. He checked the gun, glad to see that aside from the usual brush scrapes, it had been well cared for. He made sure it was fully loaded, then racked a round into the chamber.

He lowered the hammer to half-cock, and setting the

carbine on his right shoulder, he tramped ahead cautiously, making for the back of the high, false-fronted buildings lining the south side of the main street. When he reached the back of a barber shop, he slowed his pace but continued walking up a narrow gap between the barber shop on his right and a saddlemaker's shop on his left. He came to the front of the barbershop, stopped, pressed his back against the rough pine wall, and glanced to his left along the main street.

No movement in that direction. The shops on both sides of the street appeared to be closed though Longarm saw no such signs hanging in any visible windows.

Longarm heard a man shout something from the opposite direction. He turned his head to peer eastward along the main drag.

A small group of folks had gathered around the gallows not far from the Guadalupe House. Not chancing a close scrutiny of the group—he was fairly certain who the group included—he pulled his head back quickly, turned, and jogged back down the gap to the rear of the barber shop. He ran around the rear of the shop and past several other buildings and privies and pens and woodpiles, careful not to make noise that might be heard from the main street to his left.

He didn't think he had much to worry about, because the closer he moved to the gallows, the louder the shouts emanating from that direction grew. He could hear women's angry voices, and the voices of men who seemed to be begging for their lives.

Longarm moved up another gap between two buildings, and peered around the corner of the Kelly Mercantile. The gallows were just beyond the store, on his side of the street. There were three men atop the gallows, with nooses around their necks, hands tied behind their backs. A closer scrutiny told Longarm they were the three town councilmen—Madison Pringle, Angus White-hurst, and Mortimer Braun. Pringle's left arm was in a cotton sling. The men were weeping and begging for their lives while another man—Bart Spicer—was being dragged away from a buckboard ranch wagon by two men in dusty range garb.

Three of the Four Horsewomen of the Apocalypse were standing in a broad arc between Longarm and the front of the gallows while a third—the demonic sister of Matilda Pringle—stood atop the gallows, cradling a brass-framed Henry repeater in her arms. She stood with one hip cocked and a smug, self-satisfied expression on her pretty face. She gave no reaction at all to the screams of her sister, who was down on her hands and knees on the other side of the street, in front of the hotel, pleading for the lives of her husband and the other men.

The demon bitches' four horses were tied to the hotel hitchrack. The ranch wagon, in which they must have hauled Spicer to town after burning the Tres Pinos head-quarters, was parked nearby.

Aside from Mrs. Pringle, there was no other towns-person in sight. Likely all were cowering beneath their kitchen tables hoping the Four Horsewomen of the Apocalypse didn't draw a bead on them.

There was quite a commotion suddenly as the hang-ing time was obviously growing near, with the three men on the gallows yelling and sobbing and Bart Spicer rag-ing and pumping his fists as two of his men half dragged and half carried the crippled ranch manager up the four gallows steps at the point of the demon women's rifles. The wheat blonde, Emma, seemed to be getting the brunt of his red-faced tirade, since she'd lured him into a phony marriage, meaning only to fuck him, ruin him, and kill him.

By the blood on the man's face and chest, they'd beaten him with a horsewhip or quirt. Emma's back faced Longarm, but by the casual way she stood watching her husband being wrestled onto the platform and then positioned under the fourth noose, she was likely sneering.

Crouched at the end of the mercantile's front gallery, Longarm quickly riffled through his options. He could fairly easily shoot one or two of the three women facing him, but the brunette on the gallows stood dangerously near the lever that would drop the trap doors beneath the condemned men's feet. As Queenie was partly obscured by Whitehurst and Braun, he didn't think he could hit her from this distance.

He looked up at the large wooden bulk of the mercantile. He'd remembered seeing a couple of windows in the second story overlooking the gallery roof and the street. Quickly, he retreated through the gap and turned to a door set in the mercantile's back wall, two steps off the ground.

He opened the screen door and flipped the metal latch of the inside door, relieved to see the door fall away from the jam. After Kelly's so-called wife had fucked him to death, his bereaved widow had apparently seen no reason to lock the place. She'd gotten all she'd wanted from the man—his savings and the dynamite he'd ordered for the miners.

The door opened into a storeroom that smelled of cured meat and molasses. To the right was a stairway. Longarm mounted the steps, lunging three steps at a time, and found himself at the top staring down a shabby hall, with a curtained doorway on either side. Beyond was a shabby living area—a kitchen with a crude wooden table, a cookstove, and a parlor outfitted with a few sticks of ancient furniture arranged around an oval hemp rug dyed red, white, and green. Beyond were two windows.

Longarm ran to the far wall and peered out the left window, which gave him a good view over the shake-shingled gallery roof onto the street and the gallows. His heart thudded.

The three councilmen were wailing, and down on his hand and knees, Bart Spicer was still throwing curses down at his lovely, grinning bride while the brunette, Queenie, caressed the wooden trap door lever with a calfskin-gloved hand.

"You girls ready to pull our picket pins and ride the hell out of here?" she called to the girls on the street above the screamed pleas of the three councilmen and the continued shouted insults of the ranch manager.

"*Sí, sí!*" gleefully yelled the Mexican, Bibi Velasco Whitehurst, while the banker shouted pleas at the dusky-skinned vixen who'd betrayed him.

"Throw the lever!" Emma Peeters Spicer shouted, cupping a hand to her mouth.

Longarm heaved the window up and snaked his carbine outside, clicking the hammer back to full cock.

Before he could settle the unfamiliar carbine's sights on the brunette's forehead, she threw the lever forward. All four men dropped out of sight beneath the floor of the gallows platform.

Matilda Pringle screamed.

Hoping the dead cowboy's carbine was sighted in

properly, Longarm drew a bead on the closest rope that hung straight down from the crossbeam. The rope moved slightly as Spicer jerked out of sight beneath the platform.

Blam!

The rope broke.

Longarm quickly ejected the spent cartridge, levered a fresh one into the carbine's chamber, and planted the sights on the next rope.

Blam!

The second rope broke.

Longarm kept his concentration on his shooting but was vaguely aware of the brunette dropping to a knee atop the platform and looking around wildly, shouting. The other women were shouting now, too, scrambling around and whipping their gazes toward the mercantile to get a fix on the shooter. The two unarmed men from Tres Pinos ducked and covered.

Blam!

The third rope only frayed.

Longarm went to the next one, and missed it cleanly.

The demon bitches started opening up on him, slugs hammering the window frame, one bullet smashing the pane just above his head, which he was sticking out the window along with his carbine. He cursed, racked another round.

Blam!

The fourth rope broke.

Rifles popped below.

Longarm did not look at the shooters or react to the bullets spraying wood slivers around his face. He took aim at the third rope but held fire when the remaining strands gave way and dropped out of sight beneath the gallows, the end tied to the crossbeam dancing free.

As a witch-like screech sounded from the platform and a bullet carved a burning furrow across his left cheek, Longarm dropped the barrel of his carbine, and drilled the brunette's right shoulder.

She squealed and flew backward, throwing her rifle off the platform.

He dove forward through the window, hit the roof of the mercantile porch on his shoulder, and rolled, rifles roaring from below and hot lead continuing to curl the air around him and pepper the mercantile wall behind him.

One slug tore across his upper right arm.

He heaved himself to his feet. The three demon women were firing their Winchesters from their knees, forming an arc around the front of the gallows, all three screaming and laughing like moon-crazed banshees. Longarm suppressed his natural male revulsion at shooting women, and fired the carbine from his right hip, levering and firing and firing again, until all three witches lay sprawled on the street, blood pumping from .44-caliber wounds in their chests and bellies and heads.

The strawberry blonde groaned and tried dragging herself over to where she'd dropped her rifle. Longarm pumped a round into the back of her neck, finishing her.

During the dustup with the other three, he'd lost track of the husky-voiced brunette. Now he saw her, swinging up into the saddle of her Appaloosa at the hitchrack across the street. She swung the horse out away from the hotel's hitchrack, and turned it east.

"Hyahh!"

"Queenie!" Matilda Pringle shouted.

The last surviving female killer rammed spurs against

the gelding's flanks and lunged along the street, heading from Longarm's left to his right and narrowly missing her sister, who was still kneeling on the street as before. Longarm raised the carbine, tracked the girl as she headed toward him and the gallows, and squeezed the trigger.

The hammer clicked on an empty chamber.

For a sixth of a second, he considered his Colt, but he doubted he'd be able to hit a moving target from this distance. Instead, he threw himself off the mercantile roof, landing atop the gallows flat-footed.

Feeling the concussion exploding up from his ankles into his jaws and ears, he ran forward. Just as the brunette was about to race past the gallows, he launched himself, managed to hook an arm around her upper torso as he flew on over the lunging pinto.

He hit the street hard, rolling, glancing back to see the brunette hitting the street just as hard, and rolling nearby, her hair, arms, and legs flying. She came to rest on her back about six feet to Longarm's right. Her breasts rose and fell as she dragged air in and out of her lungs.

"B-Bastard!" she shrieked, staring skyward. "They deserved all this!"

"Yeah, I reckon they did," Longarm said between his own ragged breaths. He glanced at the girl, sobbing with fury, full lips quivering. "But it wasn't your call. And you went too damn far."

"You!" she screamed, pushing herself to a sitting position and grabbing the Remington from its holster thonged low on her chap-clad right thigh. "You ruined everything, you bastard!"

She swung the gun toward Longarm.

But his own gun was in his hand. Aiming from a half-sitting position, he squeezed the Colt's trigger, his slug punching her straight back in the dust.

Her chest fell still. Blood gushed from the wound to dribble into the street. Her feet twitched, her head turned to one side, and she was dead.

Matilda Pringle walked over and stared down at Longarm and then at her dead sister. She dropped to her knees. Tears rolled down her cheeks. She fingered the gold locket hanging down her bosom.

"I'm sorry," Longarm said.

She shook her head. "I couldn't stop her. Try as I might, I couldn't. She was . . . very strong-willed." Matilda sobbed, shook her head again, then glared at the men beneath the gallows. "In a way, I guess I didn't really want to!"

"Oh . . . oh, God," an unfamiliar male voice said.

Longarm saw the minister he'd seen earlier, Reverend Walters, come running from the direction of the church. A tall, pewter-haired man in a white collar and black wool vest, he was staring down in horror at the dead brunette.

"Oh, Lordy, no—*my Queenie!*"

Another husband accounted for. Longarm hadn't recognized the man's so-called wife in the frumpy black outfit she'd worn at Jack Kelly's funeral.

Longarm followed Matilda's gaze to the ground beneath the gallows. All four of the condemned men were still alive though down and breathing hard, massaging their necks. Bart Spicer was on his back, flinging his torso right and left above his useless legs. He was still red-faced and raging.

"Double-crossing bitches!" the Tres Pinos owner raged.

He turned his head, locked stares with Longarm. "Thank God you got 'em."

Fury welled up like a volcano in Longarm. He raised his pistol, aimed at Spicer's leathery forehead. "I got five more pills in this six-shooter, you conniving sonofabitch. By rights, I oughta drill you twice and give these three privy snipes the rest!"

The other three men flung themselves belly down in the street and covered their heads with their arms, cowering like chicken-killing dogs.

Longarm heaved himself to his feet. While the minister crouched over her dead sister, Matilda Pringle rose, too. Draping his arm around her shoulders, the federal lawman began leading the dazed and bedraggled woman back to her home.